HEARTBLAZER

Pyrats and Potions

Heartblazer

By

Stuart Purcell, 2015

Pocket Watch Publishing

CHAPTERS

If there is magic on this planet, it is contained in water.

Loren Eiseley

For John

Prologue

The girl pulled the amber comb gently through her hair. It hung softly on her shoulders, certain wisps shining like gold in the firelight. Fully aware she was being watched she set about finishing what she was asked to do and so reattached the comb making a neat knot. Carefully she placed the jar onto the stone table and with nimble fingers added the final ingredient. She felt like her mentor's eyes were watching her every move, willing her to make an error. With trembling hands she took the long, metal spoon and mixed the potion, a spinning swirl emerging in the centre of the liquid. The girl finished and presented the jar to the watching figure.

"Are you certain you have mixed it correctly?"

"I think so," muttered the girl, now doubting herself a little. *Potion mixing was not as easy as it seemed, one wrong ingredient added at the wrong time might seem like a trivial mistake but wait until you go to use the concoction for its purpose, you'll be surprised, you may even be shocked, so shocked that you will regret ever having tried to make a potion in the first place.*

"This needs to be perfect every time it is made or it will fail to work," barked the mentor. The girl sealed the jar with a wood-carved lid and twisted it shut.

"I hope it works. I think it should, can we test some of it?"

"No, don't be foolish, it requires one more element to complete it. We need to keep as much of it as we can and wait until the time is right."

"When will that be?" The girl walked to a stone cabinet and reaching up stored the jar safely on a shelf.

"Don't worry, my dear. When the time comes, I'll call on you to help and you'll know what to do. But for now sit next to me and let's watch the fire burn out." The girl sat. The teacher patted and stroked the girl's golden hair until she drifted off to sleep.

Chapter 1

End of Summer School

Summer school!! Who invented such a thing? After spending a whole year in school, learning and trying your best, to be expected to go and take dreary lessons during the summer holidays was a cruel punishment—this was exactly how Michael felt. His mum had enrolled him in three weeks of extra lessons because his maths wasn't up to scratch. He really wasn't enjoying them one bit; he would have much preferred to hang out with his dog. *But never mind,* he thought, *it's nearly finished and then I can really enjoy the summer.*

He ran as fast as he could, his feet barely touching the footpath. It was the last day of summer school and he was late.

"You're not usually so eager to get to class!" Startled, Michael turned his head. It was Evie, the girl from across the street. Evie had been watching Michael carefully over the last week and couldn't help but notice the glum face he wore every day. He didn't answer her. He kept himself well hidden beneath his Dublin cap. She tried again.

"Are you doing anything interesting next week when summer school is over?" Michael made a rather

3

strange noise, somewhere between a grunt and a wheeze, readjusted his cap so the peak was angled to the ground but spoke no actual words. Evie swept a handful of hair away from her face and sped off in front, leaving him alone. A little surprised, he stopped and watched her fluorescent trainers hop on the footpath until she disappeared around a corner. *Had he been too rude, he wasn't sure?*

Up until now, he had managed to get by with saying very little to her during all of summer school. She was a nice enough girl and this wasn't the first time she had tried to chat with him but you see, for some time now, Michael preferred his own company. He had succeeded at avoiding all the children in summer school; he even managed to stay clear of Dmitri. This was quite a feat as Dmitri was not an individual you could easily avoid.

Michael had always felt Dmitri was everything he was not; Michael was pretty short with lean arms and legs. On his head you could find an untidy nest of hair. From a distance he could be mistaken for a scarecrow. A scarecrow was quite fitting to Michael not only for his appearance but also for his desire to remain silent when spoken to. In contrast, Dmitri was tall and as broad as a wardrobe with slick, treacle-coloured hair. Dmitri was not quiet. He was loud and brash and somehow couldn't help being at the centre of every drama.

Michael reached the school just in time, the sound of the bell still hanging in the air. In the yard, some students were left throwing basketballs, trying to get one last one through the hoop. Dmitri was in the middle of the court with his back to the hoop. He used his thick arms to hurl the basketball over his head aiming for the net. Sure enough, the ball smashed against the backboard with great force and fell neatly through the hoop onto the tarmac before bouncing to a stop. The other boys whooped and cheered for him. Michael passed by them. He kept his eyes on the ground as he hurried into the school. Steps behind him, he could hear the boys following in, still applauding Dmitri's success.

Michael couldn't keep his eyes off the clock yet only twenty minutes had passed.

"Michael, can you please photocopy this sheet for me?" called the teacher from the top of the room. He suddenly sat upright trying to look interested. Michael was only too glad to leave the classroom for a few minutes; he was thoroughly fed up with fractions. He gave Miss Meehan a false smile.

"How many copies should I make?" he asked. The teacher walked down to his desk.

"I need about 12, yes 12 should do it, thank you Michael." Then she lowered her voice. "I need you to do something for me; could you find Dmitri and bring him back here please. He left to use the bathroom a half an hour ago and he's still not back." Michael nodded and got up to leave. "You can go on your way back from the photocopying room," she added, smiling eagerly.

The photocopier was in a room no bigger than the average bathroom. Michael pushed the door and walked in. The door slammed behind him. The room had very little light in it; a grubby blind covered a tiny window blocking out the summer sun. The yellow walls were chipped. Michael opened the lid of the photocopier and slid the sheet of paper on the glass panel. He punched in the number of copies he needed and hit the start button. The machine whirred into action and its light briefly filled the room with a curious green glow. Michael was lost in a daydream— hypnotised. He happened to look over his shoulder and immediately let out a cry of both surprise and fright. Dmitri was standing in the corner of the room with his back against the wall and his head touching the base of a shelf.

"What are you doing here?" he whispered through gritted teeth. He looked agitated, his eyes darting about in their sockets.

"Miss Meehan asked me to photocopy some stuff," replied Michael, "what are you doing here, I thought you were going to the toilet?"

"I was on my way to the library when I heard old Sykes whistling and coming this way so I hid." Mr Sykes was the caretaker of the school. He was old, he was grumpy and it seemed as if he enjoyed getting students into trouble. He was a sour puss about most things students got up to in the school but his biggest peeve was when students entered the library unaccompanied by an adult.

"Meehan sent me to look for you," said Michael. "Why?" asked Dmitri, peeking out into the corridor, his nose nearly getting squashed between the door and its frame.

"She's wondering what's keeping you." Dmitri said nothing but continued to stare out the door. He bit his lip, his front two teeth twitching like a jackrabbit.

"Why are you so jumpy?" asked Michael.

"I'm not jumpy," Dmitri replied, "I just want to go to the library for a look around." Michael narrowed his eyes suspiciously. *A look around...in the library. He didn't believe him. What was Dmitri really up to? Something he shouldn't?* It was the last day of summer school and Michael planned on getting through it without causing himself any trouble, so maybe he should keep his nose out. Then again, he felt since he came upon Dmitri in hiding he had a right to know what he was up to.

"What do you need in the library?" he asked casually. Dmitri remained silent for a heartbeat then jerked his head out of the door followed by his lanky body.

"I'm outta here," he said running down the corridor.

"Come back!" shouted Michael.

The taller boy was too fast and had disappeared up the stairs to the library on the first floor before Michael could catch his breath. Michael climbed the stairs in twos and with heaving shoulders finally burst through the library door demanding answers. "Why are you in here?" he shouted.

"Keep your voice down. Sykes is on the prowl and he'll hear us; he doesn't like us in the library on our own."

"Just tell me why you're here. Why all the secrecy?"

"Never mind what I'm doing here. I think you should head back to Meehan's and out of my way." Dmitri stood with his feet squarely apart, one index finger pointing in Michael's direction. Michael was persistent. "Tell me what's so great about the library?" Dmitri didn't move, completely ignoring the other boy. Michael continued, "You're not usually so interested in books. You know these books have more words than pictures." A smirk twisted along Michael's lips. This was too much for Dmitri's patience and he charged at Michael.

Realising there was nowhere safe to run, Michael immediately regretted his insolent words. With no other choice, he leaped over a trolley of books but misjudged his athletic ability and landed on the floor, books spilling on his head. Dmitri was taken by surprise by this move and he too ran into the trolley and flipped over the top of it landing on the floor. Both boys lay in a mess of novels, dictionaries and atlases. Michael scrambled about looking for his cap. He retrieved it and replaced it on his head.

"What's the racket in here? Who's making all that noise?" Sykes, the caretaker stood in the doorway; he wasn't whistling now, he was fuming. He eyeballed the boys and barked at them.

"What are you two doing in here? Get down the stairs, the pair of you. You've got some explaining to do to Miss Meehan!"

Chapter 2

A Game of Rounders

"I really can't believe it Michael. You've never been in trouble for fighting in school before. Tell me again what happened." Michael was trying to eat his dinner in peace but his mum kept interrupting it, firing questions at him. Joan Devoy was softly spoken on normal days but this wasn't one of those days; she was cross with Michael and so her voice was loud and harsh and not at all sweet and motherly.

"I told you it was an accident. I tripped over in the library. I wasn't really fighting," he groaned as he swallowed the last mouthfuls of dinner.

"An accident it may have been but your teacher made you stay back and tidy the library. You must have made quite a mess. You and that other boy. What is his name again? I really wish—"

"He's called Dmitri."

"You shouldn't be fighting Michael, it's not right. You should meet Dmitri and make peace with him." Michael stood up from the table and dropped his plate into the sink.

"We weren't fighting and I'm not going to make peace with him. I'm glad I don't have to see him for the rest of the summer." Joan watched her son exit the kitchen. He walked with a hunch, slamming the door behind him. She slumped down in a chair and exhaled heavily. She was used to this behaviour. She had witnessed it on and off for the last two years. *How could she help her son feel happier?*

Just then there was a soft scratching on the back door. Joan opened the door and in trotted a copper-coloured spaniel with bright eyes and a tail that shook happily.

"You hungry Penny?" Joan spooned some dog food into a metal bowl and placed it on the floor. She watched the dog fondly; she was such a lovely dog, a true family member, pleasant and trustworthy. Penny thrust her head into the bowl and chewed hungrily, spilling it as she went. *You don't have very good table manners though do you,* thought Joan.

Penny had been a present to Michael from his parents two years ago for his tenth birthday. Michael loved the dog and spent as much time as possible with her. The dog, you see, reminded him of his father. Just after Michael was given Penny, Michael's mum and dad decided that they would live separately so now Michael lived with his mum in Dublin while his dad lived in England. His dad came to see him often but not often enough for Michael; his dad always seemed to be working. Michael never really spoke about how he missed his dad but Joan knew that was the main reason for his unhappiness, why he hadn't any real friends and why he always seemed to be cross about something or other. She wished she could spend more time with him but she worked long shifts at the local hospital and now to make matters worse she had no choice but to work for the next two weeks instead of taking Michael and Penny away on holidays. He wasn't going to like that, she was certain.

Michael sat at the foot of his bed. His eyes were red from frustrated tears. Whenever he was upset, he always seemed to think of his dad. Two years later and he still missed him. He felt empty inside. *Why did things have to change? This bedroom held so many memories of him*. On the walls were photos of Michael and his dad together. One photograph showed Michael with a goofy face as he held a slimy pike in his hands. He cast his mind back and recalled how much fun that fishing trip had been. On the chest of drawers was his chess set. There was many an evening Michael would try and beat his dad, getting a little more confident with each game. His dad won most of the time but once Michael got very close to being victorious. He picked up a medal he had won for swimming. It was made of shiny metal and on it was the engraved figure of a swimmer splashing through a swirl of water. Michael's dad coached him every Saturday morning and helped him learn his most feared swimming stroke, the butterfly. The butterfly is always the last stroke and the most difficult one a swimmer learns and Michael was determined to master it. And with the help from his dad, he did master it, coming first in the local competitions. He was thrilled with the win; he never stopped grinning all week. His dad beamed with pride when he received his medal. *Happy times*, thought Michael.

Michael looked up as the bedroom door clicked opened. His mum gazed down at him, smiling. She had time to gather her thoughts and figured it best on this occasion not to scold him for his yelling and his unacceptable behaviour. Joan decided to forget about the incident and focus on just talking to her son and making up with him. She couldn't change what had happened. What's done was done.

"Are you alright?" she asked, her voice almost a whisper. Michael blinked the tears away.

"I'm sorry for shouting," he said.

"That's okay love." Joan knelt on the floor in front of her son and gently removed his cap. She ruffled his sandy mop.

"I'm not annoyed about what happened at school anymore," she said. "I worry about you. I need to know that you're happy. When you get into trouble I'm always afraid it's caused by bad behaviour—bad behaviour that happens because you're feeling sad or angry."

Michael looked at the floor, his eyes getting teary again. "I miss my dad. Why can't he just live here?" he whispered.

"You know he has his reasons Michael. He would if he could. He said he's coming to visit at some point during the summer." This good news had no effect on the boy. Michael put his cap back on, its peak covering his puffy eyes.

"I think I'll go to bed," he said.

"Before you do, I have to tell you something... and you're not going to like it."

"What?" Michael stared at his mum, ready to argue about whatever news she was going to share.

"I have to work this next two weeks so we won't be able to go on holidays... and I can't leave you on your own."

"No holiday?"

"I'm afraid not. We can go another time, the summer is only starting!"

"What do you mean you can't leave me on my own. I'm twelve years of age, I'll be fine."

"I've just enrolled you in a summer camp which starts in school next Monday."

Michael fell back on the bed and pulled the cap down, covering his entire face. Either side of him, his fists were bunched like two grenades waiting to explode. "I've only just finished summer school which I hated and now I have to go to a stupid *summer camp*. I'm not going. Thank you for ruining my summer. If you're trying to make me happy, this is not the way to do it."

"I'm sorry Michael," said Joan standing up. "I will do my best to make it up to you but I've paid for the summer camp and you *will* go to it." His mother calmly walked out of his room leaving him lying on his bed in a cloud of anger.

Well here he was again, facing another day at school doing things he didn't feel like doing, being forced to play with kids he'd prefer not to and missing out on spending time with Penny. He figured Penny would feel really abandoned since he spent so much time away from her and then he remembered something his dad told him about dogs; that they would always remain devoted, no matter what. The thought of his dad caused him to smile. *Be positive* Michael told himself. Maybe he should just make the most of this summer camp; *how bad could it be?*

Michael walked into the school hall for registration and immediately crashed into the towering figure of Dmitri. His face aghast, Michael stopped in his tracks, his mouth hanging open in an 'o' shape. Dmitri glared.

"Oh no, not you," he said. "Do you know I'm here at this summer camp because of you? If you hadn't followed me into the library the other day, none of this would be happening."

"I don't see how I'm to blame for you being here." Michael glared back.

"Well, genius," said Dmitri, "my parents have decided I could learn some personal responsibility by taking part in this summer camp instead of going away on a surfing holiday with my cousins. So thanks to you, I'm stuck here!"

At first Michael said nothing then as Dmitri walked off he called to him, 'I don't want to be at this stupid summer camp either." At that very moment the hall just happened to be less noisy than usual and everyone, including the teachers heard Michael's outburst. The walls suddenly felt like they were moving away from, leaving him all alone in the centre of the hall, dozens of eyes staring at him in silence. Michael scanned the room and was met with stern faces and shaking heads. He had let himself down, he felt awful.

After a morning of arts and crafts Michael was glad it was lunch time. He still felt so embarrassed. He found a quiet spot in the corner of the basketball court and settled down to eat alone. After a few minutes, he was surprised to see Evie walking towards him. *She hadn't mentioned coming to summer camp.* She was bouncing a small, rubber ball with one hand and sucking on the remains of a pear with the other.

"Can I sit down?" she asked.

"If you want" said Michael. He drummed his fingers on the top of his knees. He was feeling uncomfortable. "Don't worry about this morning," Evie reassured. "You saying that was kinda funny. I bet there are more than you who wish they were off on holidays with their families instead of being here."

"Were you supposed to be on holiday with *your* family?" Michael inquired.

"Yes, I was but now my parents have to work. So I'm stuck here too."

"The same thing happened to me," sighed Michael. "My mum's a nurse and she has to work so we can't go on holidays. I'm also fed up 'cause I'd much prefer to be at home, playing with my dog."

"Oh dear," Evie chuckled, "we are a funny pair you and I...feeling sorry for ourselves." The bell to mark the end of lunchtime rang out and Evie jumped up to her feet. "Come on," she shouted enthusiastically, her eyes shining, "let's just make the most of it while we're here. We're playing rounders next and I have a mean throw."

The teams for rounders were decided by Miss Meehan who had signed up to run the summer camp as well as teaching maths for summer school. She was a dedicated teacher who had a reputation for being fair so it only fitting that she take on the role of referee too. Michael was quietly content to see Evie on his team. *Why had she been so nice to him when he had been so rude to her before?* Maybe he should give Evie a chance. Since he was stuck here at summer camp, perhaps it would be good to have a friend. He made a mental note to be nice back to her.

It was the most perfect summer day; gulls swooped in long zigzags across the open sky, a warm breeze tickled the clover and the buttercups making them dance. In spite of his grumpy mood and his wanting to be alone, Michael had to admit that he was quite enjoying himself. The game was fun and so far he realised he was rather good at it; he even managed to make a home run.

Everything was going superbly until he had another encounter with Dmitri. It was Dmitri's turn to bat and Michael found himself in the position of bowler. The two boys stared at each other across the field, Dmitri gripping the bat with his claw-like hands, Michael lazily rolling the ball between his palms. They were ready to play. Michael raised his hand over his head to take aim but then stopped. He just stood there.

"Come on!" cried Dmitri. "What are you waiting for?" It was at that point that Michael realised he was able to bat quite well but he wasn't terribly good at throwing and with everyone watching on he hesitated. Seconds passed and the other children started yelling at him to hurry up. What should he do? He felt embarrassed for the second time that day. Dmitri kicked his heel into a bare patch of soil and again shouted. "Come on! You're holding up the game."

"Please give him a chance," called Miss Meehan. Michael rolled his shoulders and made a decision. *I have to just go for it*, he mused. At last, he took aim and threw. The ball flew about three metres and fell short half-way between the boys. Chewing his bottom lip, Dmitri did his best to control his frustration. He held his gaze with Michael but didn't shout. The other children were now getting impatient too. Just then one of the other teachers waved to Miss Meehan and she jogged in the direction of the school calling, "I'll be back in a minute. Stop the play until I return."

When she was gone Dmitri shouted, "Let's play on" and Michael resumed his spot. He looked as awkward as ever.

"Let someone else throw," came a voice from the field. Evie moved towards Michael to take over.

"Let me help. I have an excellent throw," she said but he just waved his hand for her to stay back. Evie knew she was a good thrower—*as good as any boy* but she left Michael alone to try again.

"I can do it," he said.

"Well, do it and hurry up," roared a few of the children, boredom coming over them. Michael didn't hesitate this time. He leaned his right shoulder back and moved it forward in a sudden burst. The ball shot out of his hand and sped towards the waiting figure of Dmitri. It flew in a low curve close to the ground, moving quickly. Taken off guard, Dmitri fumbled to try and hit the ball but much to his dismay, missed it. The spinning ball came to an abrupt stop right between his legs.

"Eeeeouwwhh!" screamed the boy, falling to his knees and doubling over in pain. Evie and the other children ran and formed a circle around him. Some of them looked over at Michael and frowned. Michael knew he had caused more trouble. He wasn't sure what he should do so he just sat down and scraped the sole of his trainer with a twig. After a while, Dmitri rose from his position on the ground and thankfully found he was able to stand again. His face was red, his mouth an ugly line of teeth. He still had tears streaming from his eyes. "Where is he?" bellowed the boy looking around him. "What an idiot! I'm going to make him sorry he ever messed with me. Michael got to his feet and was about to say something when Dmitri grinned deviously and stretched his shoulders like a hungry lion preparing for the kill. He picked up the ball that had hit him so precisely and so painfully moments ago and as quick as lightning, launched it at Michael's face. It rammed right into his mouth—Dmitri's skills of aiming at a basketball hoop were excellent and so too were his face-hitting skills. Blood filled Michael's mouth and he spat it out on the grass. At that moment Miss Meehan noticed there was some drama unfolding and she ran to the group.

"My goodness Michael, you're bleeding. What happened?"

"Dmitri threw the ball hard at my face...and on purpose." The teacher turned to face Dmitri and dropped her lower lip in shock. "Dmitri Malinowski! Get into the office now." She turned to Michael. "You too," she snapped. Miss Meehan never usually got so angry but in light of the incident in the library on Friday, she was taking no chances with these two. Both boys started to follow the teacher across the grass and into the building.

"You are such a rat," snarled Dmitri at Michael under his breath.

"I was only telling the truth," answered Michael, "you meant to hit me."

"Of course I did, I was angry. Now I'm going to get in even more trouble with my parents, thanks to you, rat boy. You didn't even think to keep your mouth shut." The taller boy's brown eyes flickered menacingly in his head. "You'll pay for this, you rat."

Chapter 3

The Frog

It was late before Michael got home for it took some time to explain everything to Miss Meehan. He left nothing out which didn't help Dmitri's case and as such, he expected Dmitri got into pretty hot water with his parents. Luckily Michael's mother didn't ask too much about the incident. He hadn't told her the whole story—said he got a ball in the mouth but didn't say why. He had only cut his gum; his teeth were undamaged so it would likely be soon forgotten—unfortunately though, not forgotten by Dmitri. Dmitri was really annoyed with him and had said that Michael was going to pay. He didn't like the sounds of that. He should have stayed on and waited for Dmitri and at least try to apologise for getting him into trouble but he raced from the school, thankful to get away from everyone, for now they surely thought him to be an idiot and a tell-tale rat as well.

Michael lay alongside Penny on the couch, the dog's tail steadily beating against a cushion. He almost felt like asking her for advice—*what will Evie think of me now? We were just beginning to get along.* He was delighted that he didn't feel shy with Evie. She made the experience of summer camp more bearable. But tomorrow, that will all probably have changed. Penny rolled over on her back, her fluffy ears flopping out across his thigh. Michael wished he could just spend tomorrow and the rest of the summer with Penny and stay away from his school and everyone in it. What was he going to do? He had made a mess of things.

Michael's mum sat down on the couch, propped herself up with a large cushion and turned on the television. The 9 o' clock news appeared on the screen. There was a man reporting about the scarcity of Dublin's water. They both watched in silence. The reporter was standing outside a government building in the city, explaining the situation.

"It appears the city could soon have a major water crisis. Many suburbs of Dublin have found themselves with inadequate supplies. The public have been advised to not leave taps running and only use what is necessary for everyday living. Engineers and public servants are baffled, they can't understand where the water has gone..."

Michael's interest in the news quickly faded.

"I'm off to bed," he said, "I'm really tired." Getting up from his slouching position on the couch, Michael kissed his mother gingerly on the cheek and said good night. Penny wagged her tail at her pal as he left the room and then turned over to continue her lounging.

Within minutes, Michael was in bed and setting his head down on the pillow. Sleep came upon him in no time.

His eyes blinked open. Something had stirred him. He listened intently. A rattling noise——rather like teeth chattering and biting. His bed sheets felt wet. He jerked his left leg. Something ran over it, scuttling to a sudden stop. He reached out his hands and touched wet fur and a cold long tail——*rats!* There were several of the furry creatures in his bed. He bit his lip and could feel some dry blood still lodged there from the game of rounders. *Was this real?* Panicking, he sat up. He tucked his legs under him and reached out a hand, struggling to switch on his bedside light. As soon as the light came on, a dozen or so rats leaped and landed on his face and head, their gnawing teeth scratching at his cheeks and nose. The rattling noise turned into words. It seemed as though the rats were chanting, chanting the same word over and over again through their horrible, yellow teeth.

"Rat, rat, rat, rat." Michael began to cry out but found he had no voice. Was he going out of his mind? "RAT, RAT, RAT, RAT, RAT!"

He woke in a cold sweat with his pillow over his head. He was thankful he had been dreaming. His heartbeat relaxed. He watched his curtains fluttering in the black night air next to the open window. He lay still for some time just listening to his breathing until his ears were teased by another noise. It was, (he was happy to admit) nothing like the noises he had heard in his dream. It was a peculiar sound, just like a croak but there was something else. *What was it?* It reminded him of bells—little jangly bells. Both sounds were produced at the exact same time, creating a strange blend. They appeared to come from the back garden. Ensuring himself that this was actually happening, Michael jumped up out of bed and tiptoed to the window to investigate.

At first, there was nothing strange to see. He had a pretty good view over the garden thanks to the brightness of the surrounding street lights. Then he saw something moving slowly. It was glowing green and was somehow unnatural and unlike anything Michael had seen before. He grabbed a small torch from his bedside locker, a thick jumper and his cap. Pulling the jumper over his head, he made his way downstairs. Penny jumped from her basket in the kitchen and followed him out the back door. She was quite eager to join in this nocturnal outing.

The garden was very still. They jogged to the back wall. The green glow had disappeared. Using his feet, Michael searched for it through the shrubs and bushes. Penny ran in circles, every now and again stopping to sniff about. She was delighted to be out with her pal who had never taken her out the back garden to play in the dark before. Michael was beginning to think that he may have been mistaken; that the green glow he saw from his bedroom window was perhaps nothing more than his imagination. The garden remained very calm, very silent. He was about to leave when the croaking and bells began again, louder and clearer. The dog whimpered and stuck her nose under the shed, searching in true doggy fashion.

'Is it under there Penny?" Michael joined Penny on the ground and shone the torch in the gap between the soil and the shed. He could see nothing but yet the odd noise continued.

Without warning, a bright green, bloated frog jumped from nowhere and landed on Penny's back. The dog immediately jerked this way and that, howling as she went.

"Stay calm girl," Michael whispered, his face alive with excitement. He kept his eyes on the strange-looking creature. It seemed pretty harmless so he decided to try and catch it. "Stay still Penny," he whispered again. The dog however did not heed Michael's request and began spinning, her shape a fuzzy brown blur. She was like a giddy goat, craning her head backwards excitedly to try and catch the slimy passenger in her teeth. The frog got louder still. Penny joined the racket, barking with glee. She was enjoying this game.

"Slow down, stop!" he called to her but she continued to whirl round and round, howling louder and louder. Lights appeared in the surrounding houses. Not knowing what else to do Michael caught hold of the dog's tail to try and make her slow down. Somehow, this worked and Penny suddenly stopped. There sat the frog, not moving a centimetre. Michael took his chance. He leapt at the frog and somehow caught it cupping his hands around its throbbing body. Penny wriggled beneath his feet causing him to fall flat on his face. But Michael didn't care—he had it. The creature was throbbing more wildly. Michael felt that his fingers were strangely hot and tingly but that didn't stop his steadfast hold of the frog.

Awoken by the commotion, the next door neighbours wandered outside in their pyjamas calling, "Who's there?" Mrs Devoy came out too. She shuffled across the lawn in her slippers. Michael's concentration was momentarily broken. He released his grip slightly and the glowing frog bounded away from him and made its escape through a tiny gap at back of the flower bed.

"Drat!" said Michael thoroughly annoyed with the new spectators. "I had it! I had it!"

"Michael, are you okay?" asked his mother, pulling the cords on her dressing gown tighter around her waist. "What's going on?"

"Nothing!" called Michael innocently. He had rolled over on his back and Penny was licking his cheek affectionately.

"Are you okay? Why are you out here?" Joan Devoy bent down to her son, genuinely worried. He sat up and looked at her, a grin plastered on his face. "I'm fine," he insisted, "just thought I saw a rat."

Chapter 4

A Boat Trip

It was another beautiful morning, the sky cloudless, tinged with orange and purple. Evie was walking next to Michael on their way to the school.

"I'm surprised you showed up today, after the trouble you caused yesterday."

"I didn't start it," he muttered.

"I know that but you could have just pretended that the ball hit your face by accident."

"He was out to hurt me," said Michael. Evie was not convinced.

"You should try and make it up to Dmitri. He's really quite nice, once you get to know him." Michael screwed up his mouth as if he had just eaten a wedge of lemon, skin and all.

"I won't be saying anything to Dmitri Malinowski. In fact, I'll be staying well clear of him. He has never liked me and never really given me a reason to be his friend. I have no interest in talking to him."

Evie stopped walking and faced Michael. She decided to be brutally honest.

"You are not Mr Popular right now," she announced. "You ruined the rounders game for everyone yesterday, and now the teachers think that we're all out to make trouble. You've also got Dmitri into hot water with his parents and our field trip today was nearly cancelled because of you and Dmitri... and all the fighting. The teachers are afraid that you are going to start up another argument as soon as you can. Maybe you should just stay clear of everyone." Evie raised her eyebrows, waiting for a response. She then swept her fingers through her reddish-brown hair, shrugged and ran ahead; she didn't want to be late for the day's excursion up the Liffey.

"I'm still not apologising to him," called Michael. Evie didn't turn around to answer him; her mind was made up, she was having nothing more to do with him—Michael was bad news.

'Boats Around Dublin' or BÁD is located at Bachelor's Walk in the centre of the city. During the summer months it is popular among tourists and schools, offering trips up the river Liffey to take in the many sights along the way. After purchasing their tickets, passengers must tread along a sloping gangplank and wait for the barges on a pontoon which floats next to the quayside.

Michael stood with the other children on the pontoon silently waiting for their barge to turn up. They had been there for about fifteen minutes already.

He had brought his camera today so he had something worthwhile to do—it's not like he was going to have kids to talk to; he wasn't much liked right now. Hardly anyone had spoken to him this morning since his meeting with Evie on the way to the school. He sat by himself on the bus to the city and now here he was standing on one end of a floating bridge while his classmates waited on the other. He reminded himself that in spite of all the trouble, he preferred being alone. The thing was, Michael was now not so sure that he felt comfortable with that arrangement anymore. He wished Evie was still talking to him; he had surprised himself at how much he enjoyed chatting to her. He wanted to chat some more; he was very eager to tell her all about the glowing frog.

Michael raised his camera to his face and looked through the viewfinder, adjusting the lens until everything came into focus. He shifted his arms to the right and found Evie. She didn't know he was watching her. She was talking intently to someone, smiling and nodding her head. She looked relaxed and happy. Michael decided to make a special effort to speak to her later. He let go of the camera, allowing it to rest against his heart. For the briefest of moments Michael felt his chest swell with a peculiar, warm feeling. When he placed a hand on his breastbone, his palm tingled, his fingertips quivered with numbness. *What a weird feeling*, he thought. It lasted only a second and he soon forgot about it.

Only a little late, the boat finally arrived and all the children plodded on and took their seats. Most of them sat inside but Michael preferred to stay outside where he could take full advantage of the city with his camera.

The excursion began and went upstream in the direction of The Irish National War Memorial Gardens near Islandbridge. The tour guide began his speech about the Liffey and its surrounding areas:

"Dublin has an interesting past. The city was founded by a Christian community in 988 AD in, and around a darkly coloured pool of water. The locals named it Duiblinn from the Irish word dubh which means black and linn which means pool. This pool emerged from the joining of two rivers: the Liffey and a smaller tributary, the Poddle. The area next to the rivers formed a central point to the city and when the Vikings arrived, about a hundred years later, they celebrated the site and built a commercial and political hub around which the modern city rapidly grew. Nowadays, this dirty pool is no more. After years of drainage and reclaiming of soggy land, vast construction of roads, rail and public buildings, the pool was covered over and eventually dried up. Its ghostly

shape remains at the site of the Castle Garden in Dublin Castle. The pool may be gone but the Liffey and Poddle are still in full flow, the former rushing through the city, slicing it in two, the latter flowing under the city in red brick tunnels and steel culverts..."

The barge lazily slipped along, passing under all the bridges that spanned the Liffey. Michael liked the bridges; he felt each one had its own architectural style, its own personality. His favourite was the James Joyce Bridge which looked like a couple of oversized, white harps some giant musician had carelessly dropped and forgotten. Michael snapped pictures of each of the bridges. He counted eleven of them before they arrived at their destination.

The children walked through the War Memorial gardens and found a spot to have a picnic. Feeling a little braver about talking to Evie, Michael chose this time to approach her. Evie was sitting under a willow tree munching on an apple and reading a paperback.

"Hi Evie."

"Hi." She barely looked up from her book.

"Hey, you're right," said Michael, "I feel awful right now. Everyone's avoiding me. I've decided to go and talk to Dmitri and make things better between us."

"Sit down," she ordered. She handed him a shiny apple. "I'm glad you've calmed down and are thinking clearly. I had decided to stay away from you but then I thought that wouldn't be really fair—we all can make mistakes. We should all make more of an effort to just get along—every one of us. You should too. Do you really want to spend the next week with the other kids thinking you're an idiot? I know I would hate that." Michael bit into the apple and with juice leaking out the corners of his mouth, he smiled and said, "You're right. I would hate that too."

The pair of them sat chatting and eating in the shade of the tree for a long time. Michael told her about his Dad in England and about the encounter with the glowing frog the previous night; this really interested her.

"Did you get any photos of it?" she asked softly, afraid of anyone learning this strange information.

"No I didn't but if I see it again I'll have this baby with me!" He waved his camera back and forth in front of her face.

After getting a guided tour round the gardens from the driver of the boat, the children walked back to the jetty and everyone climbed aboard again.

"Tide must be out," said Evie crossing the small gangplank. "I've never seen it this low. I swear I can almost see the bottom of the river." Michael and Evie took their seats. The boat pushed off and straight away it was clear to all aboard, that the river was at an incredibly low level. The boat was barely moving—dragging by, every now and again skimming the top of a slimy rock. When you looked up, it seemed as if it were at the bottom of some deep trench, so far away from the edges of the city—its buildings, its pedestrians and its moving vehicles.

"If the water level drops anymore," called the driver over a speaker, "we'll just have to get out and walk!" He chuckled loudly but was stopped short because just then there was a loud crunching noise followed by a screech as stone and metal scraped against each other violently. The boat came to an abrupt stop.

"This can't be good," shouted Michael above the noise. "Come on!" He grabbed Evie by the arm and led her to the small deck outside. Just as they were dashing through the door they heard a teacher instruct the students to remain seated and not go out on deck. They ignored this and kept moving, ducking low so they wouldn't be seen.

"Evie, you're right," Michael exclaimed pointing down. "Look! You can see the riverbed!" Not much remained of the river. The boat was just managing to keep afloat. Michael was busy taking photos when Dmitri appeared on deck, also successfully sneaking out under the teachers' noses.

"You okay?" he asked Evie, ignoring Michael. "You should come inside and sit down," he advised. "You might stumble and fall if the boat jerks again." Michael removed the camera from his face.

"She's okay here with me, everything's fine."

"I wasn't talking to you," muttered Dmitri. "And you'd do well to stay out of my way."

"What's that supposed to mean? Is that a threat?" Dmitri chewed on his lip and said nothing. Michael continued, "I was going to try and make it up to you today but is there really any point? You just seem to be out to make trouble for me."

"*Me* make trouble for you? *You* have got me into heaps of trouble these last few days and I never asked for any of it." Dmitri remained calm, Michael was now starting to shout.

"Hey! I'm not the only one to blame. You're no angel." Dmitri shifted his feet shoulder-width apart and stuck out his chest.

"Calm down, why are you so angry all the time?"

"Don't ever ask me to calm down. Why are you such an annoying idiot?" Michael's face was now the colour of a clown's nose. He glared at Dmitri from under the peak of his cap, waiting for a challenge. Evie threw her hands in the air.

"Why can't both of you just shut up? You're fighting about nothing," she cried in desperation.

"Sorry Evie," said Dmitri. "It's not *my* fault someone invited a baby on this trip." Like an erupting volcano, Michael sprang from his spot on the deck and bounded at Dmitri. He was enraged and was swinging his fists at the other boy's face. Being stronger, Dmitri wrestled Michael without any effort and was able to pin him to the deck. Michael fought as best he could, sending Dmitri sliding clumsily next to him on the floor. Both boys looked a shameful sight lying and squirming like a bunch of octopuses.

"Oh look!" Evie shouted. The boys glanced her way thinking she was again pointing out their silly antics but were surprised to see she was no longer looking at them but instead was watching what was happening down below on the riverbed. Unknotting their limbs, they scrambled to the edge of the deck and peered down.

A team of the glowing frogs had surrounded the boat and were making a riotous racket. Their bodies shimmered brightly, lighting up the puddle of water that was the river, a ghoulish green.

"That's them!" yelled Michael his voice shaking with excitement. "The weird frog I saw last night but now there's so many of them."

"Wow," Evie exclaimed, "what an unusual sound they're making."

"Quick! Take some photos," called Dmitri handing Michael his camera which had come loose and fallen during their scuffle. The frogs' skin seemed to be flashing while their croaking became louder still. The river was now at its lowest and completely still. Some of the frogs disappeared below the keel of the barge while the rest made a neat line all around the base just above the waterline. Their tiny amphibious hands grasped the barge. The children gawped in disbelief at what was about to happen.

Gradually, the boat began to rock—gently at first and then, unbelievably, it seemed to lift off the riverbed, quivering and shaking like a dancing cobra.

"What are they doing?" squealed Evie. "Stop rocking the boat!" The three children did their very best to stay standing, gripping the sides of the boat, but failed, falling in a tangle of limbs on the deck. They picked themselves up and looked around. They were still the only ones there; no one else ventured outside as it was too dangerous; not even the teachers. After several minutes, the shaking slowed to a stop. The three resumed their position at the edge of the deck. Without wasting any time, the frogs began to leave. With a watery pop, they pulled their hands and feet from the boat.

Little by little, the deck filled with the other children and their teachers. They all looked confused and frightened. Dmitri, Evie and Michael didn't take their eyes off the frogs, following the line of pea-green amphibians as it vanished through a half-broken, metal grill in the quayside wall of the river.

Thankfully, the level of the water was rising again and the tour would soon make its way back to the safety of the pontoon at Bachelor's Walk.

Evie fixed her hair into place and stared at the two boys exhaling softly through a small opening in her lips. Michael was still staring at the grill in the wall. Dmitri stood shaking his head.

"That was the strangest thing I've ever seen," he whispered.

"For sure," agreed Michael. "So strange, I must find out more." He placed the cap on his lens and shoved the camera into its case, hiding all evidence of the curious, green frogs.

Chapter 5

The Plan

Michael's head was reeling. It had been quite a day, *what a field trip that was*; he had spent time chatting with Evie and it was safe to say she didn't hate him like he thought she might, he had got through the day without Dmitri and him ending up fighting again and he had seen the frog once more. But not just one frog, a whole army of them. *What strange creatures they were.*

He sat in front of his computer screen staring at the uploaded images of the grounded boat and the frogs surrounding it. He remembered how they rocked the boat while everyone on board was terrified. *Why did they approach the boat at all? Were they really trying to tip it over,* he didn't think so. And then, they vanished so quickly—*where were they off to?*

Michael was awakened from his reverie by his mum calling his name. He spun around on the chair to face her. "Earth calling Michael." She smiled at him. "How was camp today?"

"Fine, not much happened. We took a boat trip up the Liffey." He thought it best not to mention the frog situation. Not right now anyway. He wanted to find out some more before he told his mum all about it. Evie, Dmitri and he were the only ones who actually witnessed the frogs. The other children and the teachers were all too nervous to come out on deck to investigate. They weren't really sure what had taken place and when the teachers asked the three children to explain, it was with a rapid wink of an eye from Dmitri, that they all concluded the boat, more than likely, had just hit some rocky patches of riverbed and as a result, shook a little. A lie, of course...but only a little one.

"Did you patch things up with Dmitri?" His mum sat on the edge of his bed and raised her eyebrows waiting for a reply.

"Eh, yeah. Everything is fine now." He nodded intently. "Dmitri, Evie and I spent the whole day together."

"Oh I am glad," said his mum. "Evie? Is that the girl who lives at the end of our road?"

"That's her." Michael leaned back in his chair and balanced his feet on the edge of the desk where his computer sat.

"We should ask her over, for tea or something." His mum looked really pleased with herself now. "It's nice that you're starting to mix with other children your own age at last."

There was some truth in what his mother said. Joan Devoy worried about her son terribly. She had watched the decline of her son's cheerful personality ever since his father left the family home in Dublin to go and work in England. Michael was still missing his father and had shown little interest in anything but Penny his dog in quite some time. But now, he was making friends. Joan was delighted with this new development.

Michael lay in bed that night and was happy with the events of the day. His mum was right; he had made a friend in Evie and he had to admit, he was looking forward to seeing her on Monday for the second week of summer camp. *That's enough thinking for one day*, he muttered and yawning, he turned over on the mattress and made himself snug. Before sleep came upon him, he thought he felt a warm throbbing in his chest but he must have been mistaken because he drifted off to sleep in no time.

As it happened, he didn't have to wait until Monday to see Evie; on Saturday morning he spied her out on the street washing her dad's car. He made an excuse to go to the local shop for milk and stopped to talk to her on the way back.

Evie was dressed in denim shorts and a white

t-shirt. She stood and placed a hand on her hip, the other hand holding a foamy sponge.

"Morning," she called pleasantly. Michael sauntered up to her, his shoulders slouched, his face as usual, hidden under his cap.

"You're doing a good job of that car," he said.

"I'm taking this chore really seriously— doing my best because there's money in it for me." She wrinkled her nose and chuckled. "My dad thought I wouldn't be able to handle cleaning it because usually my brother does it but I insisted I could do it and I'll be happy to prove him wrong." Michael rested against a nearby wall, the litre of milk balanced in his lap. "I've been studying the photos I took the other day, those frogs are pretty amazing." Then he dropped his voice. " I think I'm going to go to the river and find out more."

"What do you mean?" asked Evie, gasping a little.

"I'm going to go and examine that gate in the side of the river. You know, the place where the frogs all went. You should come too. I'm going tonight." Evie lowered her voice even more. The front door to her house was open and she feared her parents might hear; she would never be allowed to go into the city at night.

"Into town, at night to climb into a river— are you mad?" Evie had dropped the sponge into a nearby bucket and was now standing with both hands on her hips, a look of horror on her face.

"Yes," replied Michael. "Aren't you curious to know more about those creatures. I feel like they're trying to tell me something."

"You really are mad. You think those frogs were sending you messages?"

"Maybe," said Michael, dreamily flicking the peak of his cap with his thumb.

"What about texting? Did they try and text you?" Evie guffawed at her own joke.

"Be serious," gasped Michael. "How come I got to see one of them two days in a row and no one else has ever reported seeing one—it's like they chose me...but for what, I don't know."

"And me... and Dmitri, they chose us too." Evie nodded, her head moving like a spring.

"Well, yes, " said Michael. "The three of us are the chosen ones." He stood up straight and tall leaning the carton of milk against his heart and tilting his head back in mock military fashion. "The chosen ones will investigate and conquer. Will you join me?"

"Ok," she giggled, finally convinced, "I'll go with you."

Chapter 6

Down by the River

Evie's phone flashed with a message. It was well past midnight; Michael was waiting for her outside. She trod softly downstairs trying her best not to waken anyone. Evie knew in her heart that this was something her mum and dad would not be entirely happy about—entering the city centre at night time with a boy to investigate an open grate in one of the river Liffey's quays where only yesterday after having nearly tipped over a barge, a wild group of throbbing, fluorescent-green frogs had fled. She was beginning to have second thoughts. *Why am I doing this? Adventure?* She wasn't sure. *All the signposts for adventure were pointing the one way*, thought Evie, *all I have to do is follow them.* Content with her choice to go, she continued to get ready. Pulling a warm snood around her neck and shoulders, she delicately made her escape out the side door and met Michael in front of her house.

"You've got your dog with you?" she exclaimed. Penny gazed up at her, her tongue and her tail flapping wildly. Michael patted Penny's head.

"Yeah," he replied. "She heard me leaving the house and she wanted to come. I couldn't say no."

"Cool," said Evie. "Well, let's go. I'm ready for an adventure!" The three began walking briskly, keeping their heads down and avoiding eye contact. It wasn't ideal to have two children roaming the streets of the city late at night. Michael and Evie figured if they stuck together and focused on where they were heading, they would look rather like a couple bringing their dog for a midnight stroll and would draw less attention.

"So, what's the plan," asked Evie.

"I have my camera with me," replied Michael, "I reckon we should try and get down to that gap in the wall and take some pictures—try and learn a little more about those frogs. If we're lucky, we may even see some of the little critters."

"Ok, then. Sounds good to me." Evie pulled the snood closer to her and for a second watched her warm breath drift away on the night air. Although it was summer, the evenings were cool and she was feeling chilly. " We won't be out for too long then?" she asked. "I'm eager to get back, they don't know I'm gone."

"About half an hour or so," answered Michael, "I left in secret too. If we can get some good shots then we'll just head back home straight away."

It wasn't long before the trio found themselves standing at Wellington Quay peering down at the river. This part of the city is relatively quiet at night and thankfully nobody bothered them. Michael wasted no time and started to fling his legs out over the side of the stone wall carefully guiding his leading foot onto the top rung of a metal ladder. "Wait," said Evie hastily, "you can't just climb down there."

"Sure I can." Michael continued down the ladder.

"But what about me?" Evie asked.

"You stay here with Penny. I won't be long, just a few quick shots, remember?" He waved the camera in her face, a crooked grin on his lips.

"Fine," said Evie watching him descend the ladder, "but hurry up!" She leaned against the stone and looked down at Penny. "Just you and me for a while Penny." It was too late for Evie to stop Penny; no sooner had Evie spoken, than the dog jumped up onto the top of the wall and after three seconds of assessing how far the drop was and if it was going to be a safe landing, (because dogs always consider such things), she leaped down into the darkness below. There was a mighty splash followed by Michael's surprised voice calling to his dog. Evie hung her head over the wall searching for the two of them through the chilly night air. She could just make out the white stripes on Michael's tracksuit top.

"Hey, I'm coming down too," she yelled. Without wasting any time she began the descent. Carefully crawling over the top of the wall she took one last look to make sure no one had spotted them using the ladder which she was pretty sure was only reserved for workers of the city council and not curious children.

Michael waded in the dark, murky water. It was only waist-high so he could move about with ease. He searched for Penny, trying his best to keep his camera from getting wet. Evie was perched on the lowest rung of the ladder facing out towards the river.

"Can you see her?" she called.

"No, I dunno where she is. Think I'm going to dive under."

"Is that a good idea? It could be dangerous."

"I'm a pretty good swimmer and I'm really good at holding my breath. Here take my camera." He removed the strap from around his neck and plopped the camera into Evie's outstretched hand.

"Good luck," she whispered. Michael didn't wait another second. He took a huge breath and plunged his head beneath the water.

Seconds later he resurfaced and then dipped below again. After his third try, he started to panic.

"Where is she?" he shouted frantically. It was at that moment that the glorious sound of Penny's cheerful bark was heard as a nearby echo.

"The grate!" said Evie. "She's gone through the grate in the wall." Evie pointed upstream towards the gap in the river wall. Michael stopped wading to listen.

"Oh, thank goodness she's alright." It was clear from his shaky voice that Michael was filled with relief. He loved that dog so much. After all, it was a gift from his parents and being around Penny somehow made him feel like he was around his dad. "I'll follow her," he shouted. 'You wait there!' Evie had no intention of moving. She was feeling a little uneasy now. Maybe she should have stayed home. If she had, she wouldn't have found herself shivering on the end of a metal ladder above a smelly river.

Three, five, seven minutes passed and Evie listened closely but couldn't hear Michael or Penny anymore. *Where are they*, she wondered. In the distance her eyes focused on two lights that were steadily approaching along the river. At first, she didn't give them much thought but as they grew larger, she realised what they were.

Suddenly, Michael's voice came from about ten metres away, "Evie, I found her. We're okay." He and Penny were sitting just inside the gap in the quay.

"Oh that's great. Are you coming back now?" she called.

"Yes," he shouted, "but what about the photos?" The two lights had got nearer now and were nearly upon the spot where Michael sat.

"Maybe we should just go," said Evie, "enough excitement for one night and all that." Just then, a huge barge passed Michael. It was the midnight tour of the illuminated bridges of Dublin and it was packed with giddy tourists all keen to get some interesting pictures. Luckily for Michael and Penny, they were concealed in the darkness of the opening in the quay wall.

"Evie, quick," called Michael. "Do you realise there's a barge coming your way and it's full of people. If they see you, our secret about the frogs will be out and we'll be in deep trouble. You need to jump now. The water is the only place for you to hide."

"What?" said Evie. "But I can't jump, what if I—" Splash! Evie's concentration momentarily elapsed and she slipped off the bottom rung falling into the slimy river. Caught completely off guard, she swallowed some water and the camera which was now surely destroyed hit her right in the jaw. Not concussed, she was able to rise to the surface.

"You ok?" Michael was moving towards her doing a rapid breast stroke, his chin bobbing up and down on the top of the water.

"I'm ok," she answered through watery splutters. Michael helped pull her to the grate and lifted her up to the opening where she could sit and catch her breath. The opening in the grate was probably damaged for some time now as the edges of the exposed metal were rusted and wound up with dead seaweed. Michael slipped neatly through the grating and collapsed beside Evie. He took his cap and wrung the water from it before placing it back on his head.

"So you jumped?" he asked.

"No, I slipped. I was trying to tell you I shouldn't jump because of your camera but I never got a chance to finish. I'm really sorry. It must be ruined." She touched the edge of the strap around her neck and frowned meekly. Michael was about to say that it wasn't that much of a big deal and that the main thing was that she was alright but he didn't, instead he jerked his head from side to side looking around the dark space.

"Never mind about the camera," he gasped, "where's Penny gone?"

They both looked at each other and then down the dim tunnel. It seemed Penny had gone exploring.

"Are you serious?" said Evie, "go down there. It's pitch dark." Evie was now standing, her back bent slightly as the ceiling of the tunnel was quite low. She had hung the camera on the broken grating and was tying her hair into a ponytail with her numb hands.

"I can't just leave her here." Michael was beside himself that he would lose his dog for ever.

"We can go for help, suggested Evie.

"No, she could be in real danger. We don't have time."

"But we can't see anything and I don't hear her barking." Michael picked up the camera and started to fiddle with its buttons.

"If this is still working it has a strong light on it. We could use it to find her. He shook the apparatus and a stream of water leaked out of its end.

"I think it's finished," said Evie, "let's go and get proper help." This was Evie's second time to suggest seeking help. She really didn't want to venture down a dark tunnel and especially without a light.

"No, I'm not leaving her," yelled Michael in frustration, banging the lens with his fist. The camera whirred and with a little flashing and zooming of its lens, it miraculously lit up. Michael whooped and Evie smiled at him positively, her face awash with the camera's gentle light. She could now see how much Penny meant to him. "Let's go," she said after a moment. "Let's go find your dog."

Chapter 7

The Slumber Pool

With only a moderately bright light from a camera and a sense of adventure to guide them, they marched forward to the sound of sloshing water.

It wasn't long before the tunnel narrowed and the pair moved along with more caution.

"I really hope there are no rats down here," said Michael. "I hate rats!"

"We've been walking for twenty minutes now," wheezed Evie "and we haven't heard Penny bark or make any sound. *Where could she have got to?*"

"I dunno but I'd like to keep going. The camera says the battery is at 70 percent so we'll still have light for a while."

The pair continued down the damp tunnel. Evie tried to distract her mind from the dripping walls and the low ceiling. She had a crick in her neck from stooping and her jaw was still aching from when the camera struck her. Her calves were tired and her feet were ice cold. *I should be tucked up, warm in bed*, she thought, *what if we got stuck in here and could never get out?* She so wished that the tunnel would widen. At times, it felt as if the walls were closing in on them. Michael felt similarly but was determined to be as brave as he could and keep going to find Penny. He didn't want to be negative so he didn't share his thoughts with Evie; he felt she might be only too willing to turn back if he suggested such a thing.

"It seems to be getting brighter." Michael called back over his shoulder, a flutter of hope in his voice.

"Yes, I think you're right. There's definitely light ahead." Their pace quickened with the prospect of less gloomy conditions.

Around a corner they happened on a narrow path that led up a parapet. This opened on a wide cavern. A wavy light played on the high ceiling and illuminated the steep walls. Below them was a blanket of crystal-clear water that shone and shimmered in tones of violet and green, almost like the feathers of a peacock.

"Wow! How beautiful," gasped Evie. She stared at the moving water, her eyes growing larger, her voice slurring. "I have such a need to go swimming... right now," she murmured. And with that, Evie stepped off the parapet and plunged into the pool, sinking beneath the water. Seconds later, she broke through the surface flinging her head back. Her long hair whipped out behind her like a wet rope. Michael stared down at Evie's figure encapsulated by ripples of coloured, moving water. Mesmerised, he too jumped in.

The two lay on their backs transfixed with the light above them and the swirling water around them. Neither looked at each other nor spoke. A strange haze had entered their minds and they had forgotten all previous thoughts and ideas—now all that mattered was the soothing water that enveloped their bodies. They closed their eyes, drifting to a sleepy place.

A floating human, at best needs to be fully awake to maintain a safe level of buoyancy, however some people can float safely while asleep in very still water. If your face were to slip under the surface, your brain and diving reflex would take over and cause you to waken. Michael and Evie could not rely on these safety devices since they were floating in very different water, water unlike any other water—water that hypnotised you and then tried to drag you below its beautiful but deadly surface.

The children were in a very dangerous situation; they say you lose consciousness after 2-3 minutes of being submerged and the brain dies from lack of oxygen about 4 minutes later.

Michael was the first to turn his head in this deep sleep and then sink downwards, spinning gently like a leaf. Evie quickly followed him, her arms and legs gently flapping as if she were swimming in her descent. They both dropped to the bottom of the pool lying there peacefully, their mouths curved upwards in a contented half-smile.

Chapter 8

The Glossum

It was a strange sensation, a peaceful dream that seemed to lie on top of him putting pressure all round him, followed by a faint scratching that tingled his fingers and parts of his face. Was he dreaming about rats again? This thought faded quickly for he suddenly opened his eyes and switched on his brain. He was underwater and he knew this was no dream. He felt his eyelids falling like stones and he fought to keep them up. Michael knew he didn't want to go back to that dreamy place. Again, he felt the tingle in his fingers but this time it was more painful. *Ouch*! He suddenly realised what he must do. He reached his hands above his head and used the bottom of the pool to launch himself upwards. Kicking his arms and legs as quickly as he could, he thought of how long it would be before he reached the surface and some glorious, life-giving air.

Like a spawning salmon racing upstream, he smashed through the top of the water and gasped around him hungrily. *Where am I* he wondered, his arms flying about to stop from sinking again. He felt exhausted. He dropped his head back against the water and lay there heaving, his face and chest puffing rapidly. Just then, he felt something pulling at his shoulder and felt the same tingly feeling he felt under the water. He was being dragged to the bank of the pool. A brown streak whizzed past him and jumped up onto the water's edge. Michael managed to find footing and haul himself up. He grabbed at the slippery poolside and clawed his way onto the flat surface. Finally, he collapsed beside a shivering figure. Evie—she was alive!

Evie sat up and grabbed both his hands.

"Thank goodness, you're ok," she said, her voice shaking with the cold. She rubbed his hands together. "Oh Michael, Michael, we were rescued by this guy," she said gesturing towards a creature waiting in the shadows. Michael turned over onto his belly and squinted to see it more clearly. To you and I, it most closely resembled an otter but it wasn't an otter. The creature twisted its body this way and that, its pointy tail swishing merrily at each turn. It had rather long teeth and its ears were the shape of miniature tennis racquets that twitched whenever someone spoke. Michael sat up and removed the camera from around his neck. "We were rescued by an otter?" he grunted, "I must be seeing things."

"Excuse me please, but I am not an otter!" Michael jumped to his feet in surprise, cowering and moving backwards from the talking animal.

"It's speaking," he whispered to Evie, "isn't it? I'm not going mad from almost dying, am I?"

"Yep, it's talking," Evie replied calmly. "And it talks quickly… and a lot, so keep up." She had been out of the water for several minutes now and had already become acquainted with her rescuer.

"This," she said, "is a glossum…not an otter." She turned her face towards Michael and smiled reassuringly.

"Indeed I am a glossum," the creature continued. "How could you think me anything less?" It narrowed its eyes and stood there waiting for a reply, its tail slapping the wet stone impatiently.

"Em, hi there," offered Michael, "thank you for saving us." The glossum ignored him and continued to gabble.

"Dangerous things they are, slumber pools. They draw you in with their beauty and you willingly jump in and it's all very nice and relaxing and entertaining until you begin to fall asleep and then BAM—you are at the bottom and you are drowning peacefully in a wonderful dream. I happened to be about, so I jumped in and gently nipped your fingers to rouse you from your death."

"Well, we thank you," said Evie.

"So, you're a glossum and you talk. What's your name?" asked Michael.

"Of course I talk," said the animal narrowing his eyes. "Why wouldn't I talk?" The children weren't sure what to answer. They didn't want to annoy the creature. Evie moved towards the glossum, her arms outstretched showing him she meant him no harm.

"We just meant that we've never met a glossum before and that it is lovely to meet one as nicely spoken as you." Her clever use of flattery seemed to work and the creature stopped tapping his tail and seemed calmer. It was in this quieter state that the children could see the true beauty of the creature's fur; it was luminous changing hue with the subtle movements of its breathing.

The glossum grunted, stood on his hind legs and made a mock bow.

"My name is Dvarku," he said. "And...well, as for saving your lives, I'm glad to be of service and I'm very pleased to meet you." The children chuckled with relief. They wanted to remain on his good side. Maybe he knew the whereabouts of Penny. Dvarku shifted this way and that and narrowed his eyes again.

"Why are you here?" he asked. "We've lost our dog," said Evie. " She ran down through these tunnels and we're following her. Do you happen to know where she might be?"

"The Coreland is quite a big place, a lot of caverns and tunnels. It would be very difficult to find a dog here— very difficult, but as it happens I do know where she is." Michael stood up suddenly and walked over to Evie's side.

"Where is she?" he asked, hope filling his voice. Dvarku didn't reply. Michael asked again, this time much louder. If someone knew where his dog was, he needed to know the location straight away. The longer she was missing, the harder it could be to find her.

"Tell me where she is." His yelling echoed eerily through the cavern.

"I will ask you to please not shout at me again, " hissed the glossum. I will have no part in your anger, thank you." The creature bounded about again, clearly agitated. Michael thought he had gone too far, so much so that is was unlikely the glossum would help them at all. Then, astonishingly, the creature just changed its mind. "Follow me," it said, scampering off down a trail that led away from the slumber pool.

Michael and Evie ran after the glossum through a warren of passageways. The passageways were long and dimly lit. It was an unusual light. Evie stood and examined it. "What are these?" she called to Dvarku. He stopped in his tracks to answer her. On the walls were dozens of crawling beetles. Each one's abdomen was lit up. They were humming happily, their tiny bodies creating a dull orange glow.

"They're luminobes," he answered. "They are one of our sources of light down here. As you can see, it's dark all the time so they are extremely useful insects. You should take some of them; you never know when you might need some extra light. Michael and Evie's eyes widened. *Could this place get any stranger?* They both delicately lifted up a few of the shining bugs and popped them snugly in their pockets.

"We must keep going," called Dvarku and he shot off again.

After minutes of trying to keep up with the quick-moving glossum, the three of them stopped at the entrance to a wider tunnel that had a walkway either side of an underground canal. The canal emerged from below them through cracks in the stone and flowed away towards the darkness ahead.

"Follow this path and you will find your dog," announced Dvarku. He then said nothing more and disappeared into the shadows.

The children looked at each other.

"What a weird creature and a weird place. Do you believe what he was saying?" asked Evie. "He didn't seem completely sure that Penny was down here at all. I think he's lying. Do you believe him?"

"I'm not sure. He did save our lives, we could have drowned in that pool. There's no one else here to help us. I guess we have to believe him. What other choice do we have?" Evie nodded. "We've come this far," continued

Michael, "let's keep going and hope he knows what he's talking about." And so with little else to convince them except the advice from a curiously strange creature they had just met, the two children plodded along the murky canal towards goodness knows what.

Chapter 9

Fester

Although the canal walkway was dark, the children could see quite well as hundreds of luminobes hung on the walls lighting the way. Above, some type of flying insects gently bumbled about near the ceiling, casting a gentle glow on the water below. The canal was as wide as a car from bonnet to boot and its surface as dark as engine oil.

The pair quickened their pace, eager to reach the spot where Penny was supposed to be. Michael began to wonder about his dog again; *was she trapped? Had someone or something taken her?* He hoped she was alright. Evie's mind was on other thoughts.

"I'm getting tired," she wheezed, "and hungry too."

"Just a little bit further...please," begged Michael. "After coming this far, I want to give it my best shot to try and find her." Evie agreed and they continued on.

Little by little, the air around them became damper, thicker, and it wasn't long before a heavy, green mist hung over the water, its foul stench entering their mouths making them cough. There was a strong feeling that the ceiling and walls of the tunnel were creeping in from every side but of course they weren't—instead the children's minds were sensing the foreboding atmosphere of the unknown.

Just then, the canal opened onto a large pool and a bigger cavern. The green mist was thicker here. It billowed and wrapped itself around the children. When they had adjusted to the mist and stopped coughing they stared ahead in wonder; scattered through the sheet of smelly fog were hundreds of red lights.

"Look!" cried Evie. "Lots of luminobes, they're bright red—they look awesome." The beady lights moved towards the children. Michael and Evie had taken delight in the luminobes they had put in their pockets earlier so now they welcomed the chance of coming in contact with some more. The luminobes buzzed forward, gradually fluttering into view. It was then that the children realised they had been very much mistaken.

With gnashing teeth and snarling grins, a troupe of greasy, oversized rats padded along the edge of the water. Their eyes were as red as blood. Some of them swam towards the children, their long tails skimming the canal's surface. They climbed from the water and sat at the edge, waiting. The air was filled with the horrid sound of their tiny chomping teeth.

"Oh no! Rats!" Michael's face lost all colour. He swallowed nervously. The rats moved faster now. They scurried with purpose, their eyes shining brighter still.

Evie and Michael backed against the wall in fear.

"I hate rats," yelled Michael above the din of gnashing teeth.

"Well, I'm not a fan of them either," Evie called back. "What are we going to do? I don't believe they're very friendly." Evie couldn't have been more right because just then, the rats ran at the children's legs. Their knees buckled from the force and they fell among the nasty vermin. The screaming children squirmed but it was all in vain; several of the rats twisted their tails around Michael and Evie's waists and bound them up so as they couldn't move a muscle. Gasping for breath, the captives lay on the ground terrified, as a ring of red eyes surrounded them. Just when Michael thought, *this is the moment, the rats are going to pounce on us, h*e shut his eyes awaiting impact...but it never came. Michael cautiously looked around.

A single rat entered the circle and looked down at the prisoners. He was a little larger than the others and when he walked, his soft belly jiggled about. His tail was short, branded with a white tip that made it look like it had been dipped in flour. He was thoroughly disgusting;

his most disgusting feature was the soft, empty hole that sat ugly and useless in his head where a blood-red eye had once been. The creature spoke in a rough voice.

"A pair of brats. I knew you'd bump into me sooner or later. I am Fester, the Chief Pyrat." It paused for a moment, its grin growing larger. All the other rats chattered their teeth even louder.

"Guess what? I like to take things and I have your pretty dog." At these words, Michael wriggled on the floor, frantically trying to free himself.

"Is she alright? Give her back. You better not have hurt her! If you have, you'll have me to answer to."

"I really don't think you're in a position to make threats, do you?" The rat leaned down to Michael's face stating his words precisely, his single eye focused on the boy's forehead like a deadly laser. Michael felt his eyes water at the rancid stench of the rodent's breath.

"Please let us go. We just want to get our dog and go home."

"You can go home," said Fester, "and you can have your dog, but first you have to do something for me."

"What?" shouted Michael.

"Oh please don't shout, it makes me all nervous." The rat raised his eyebrows and shivered a little, mockingly.

"What do you want?" said Michael.

"Indulge me in a little game we play down here. It's called Ratsling. It involves swimming and throwing—nothing you humans can't handle."

"No! I don't want to play your stupid game. Just let us go." The cavern suddenly fell silent.

"I thought I was being fair," snarled Fester through his yellow teeth. "Play the game with me and I give you back your dog—you all go free. However, you have now rattled my cage, my rat cage, and I don't take kindly to hearing the word no, so the deal just got a whole lot worse for you, you stupid boy."

"What are you going on about?" Michael continued to try and free himself from the binding grip of the rats' tails.

"I'll tell you what I'm going on about," said the fat rat. "Ratsling! You *will* play Ratsling with me. If you win, you get to keep your dog and go home, but if you lose—." The rat paused here, his tail twitching, "you'll become my prisoners and you'll never see your dog again." Michael lay still, his cheek cold against the ground. He had stopped wriggling.

"And if I don't play?" he asked.

"You don't want to know the answer to that." With a nasty smirk filled with mischief and in make-believe slow-motion, Fester took his white-tipped tail and swiped it across his throat in a grizzly gesture. Michael and Evie winced, Michael swallowed bitter saliva.

"What are the rules?" he asked in a defeated half-whisper.

Chapter 10

Ratsling

The rats wasted no time locking Evie up. She was forced into a large cage from its position on the floor. "You can rattle that cage all you like," Fester said as he watched dozens of rats raise the cage by means of a pulley, "but you won't get free." Escape was out of the question so instead she watched the scene below, all the time willing Michael to do his very best at this game that neither of them had ever heard of before.

Michael knew there was no way out of this. He had to take part in the game, otherwise himself, Evie and Penny were doomed. He weighed up his chances; a game with swimming—he felt he could handle that, after all, he had won medals for it. But the game also had an element of throwing. During the game of rounders, Michael had proven that he wasn't very good at throwing—*oh no*, he said to himself, *this could be worse than I thought.*

It seemed Ratsling was a fairly simple game to play; two players throw a ball, (or in this case, a tangle of heavy roots), at rats hanging from the ceiling. A player gets one point if he hits a rat, two points if he knocks it down. You must retrieve the ball by catching or swimming after it before your opponent does. The more often you get the ball, the more often you have the opportunity to throw and score points. When all the rats are knocked down, the winner is the one with the most points.

Michael took off his cap, his tracksuit top and bottoms, trainers and socks. He figured the fewer clothes he was wearing for swimming the better. He left on his shorts and his t-shirt; *goodness knows what was lying in that filthy canal.* The notion that all the water down here was stinking and foul-smelling suddenly struck him as being odd. *Why was that so?* You would have thought that water found within the ground would be the purest ever. *The exception of course being the water in the slumber pool, that wasn't dirty, it was clean but also unnatural and very deadly as well.*

Michael looked up; he hadn't noticed it before—there was a large network of roots from some plant spread out across the ceiling of the cavern. At various spots there was a greasy rat swinging upside down, its scarlet eyes piercing the darkness. Michael counted five of them. He figured if he knocked three down he had a pretty good shot of winning and getting him, Evie and Penny home.

A rat swam to the centre of the long pool and left the root ball floating there. At his end Michael stood waiting in the water. At the other end he could make out the tubby figure of Fester and his one glowing eye.

"Good luck to you, my friend," the rat hissed. Ignoring him, Michael took a moment to concentrate on what was about to happen; he wouldn't allow himself to become flustered and blow his chances at winning—there was just too much at stake.

The shrill sound of a squealing rat marked the start of the game. Michael torpedoed through the water, his eyes set on the root ball. With controlled strokes, he reached it in no time. He couldn't see Fester anywhere. Michael grasped the ball with one hand and aimed it at a hanging rat. He missed. Fester appeared on the water's surface and cleanly caught the ball. He launched it towards the ceiling and hit a rat, causing the miserable creature to fall down.

"Two points to me," he cackled. Michael was not paying attention as he already had the ball in his hands and was getting ready to throw again; he hurled it at a rat. The ball flew wide of the suspended rodent and splashed into the water. "Oh dear," said Fester, "throwing is not your strong point, is it?" Michael bunched his fists, willing himself to do better.

From her excellent vantage point above Evie cried down to him.

"Come on Michael! Concentrate on the target, focus and then aim." Michael could no longer hear her—he was beneath the water again swimming steadily, his arms and legs kicking with force. Fester was chasing after the ball too, hoping to bag another two points. Michael seized the tangle of roots and without hesitation threw it fast and long among the hanging bodies of the rats. Miraculously, he managed to knock two down.

"Yes, yes, well done Michael," screamed Evie, "four points to you!" She was on her knees and was shaking the cage with wild excitement. Michael glanced at her but then wished he hadn't; taking his eyes away from the game for a second, Fester launched the root ball straight at him. The hollow roots were as hard as metal pipes and they lashed against his face, stinging. Through his watery eyes, Michael could make out the grinning features of the horrible rodent who had just gained another two points.

"You almost blinded me," Michael shouted at the rat. "That wasn't very fair."

"Oops," said Fester. "I forgot to tell you that you can throw the ball at your opponents if you so wish. It, eh, slows them down." The audience of rats guffawed, their teeth still chomping and chattering. The din was deafening.

"Don't pay any attention to that rotter Michael," shouted Evie, "it's four all, you can do this. Come on!"

Michael was angry but didn't waste time pondering his mistake. Quick as a flash he dove into the water after the ball. He reached it easily as the rat was too busy enjoying his success to notice Michael's movements. Michael stopped and aimed for a hanging rat. He hit one but failed to knock it down. He only scored one point. In a flash, Fester grabbed the ball. Michael was on the move again.

"Five-four, you're winning Michael, come on, you can do this!" Evie's encouragement rang through his ears. *She was right, I can do this and send us all home. I'm an excellent swimmer,* he remembered, *and my throw is getting better.* He shook himself from his reverie ready to catch the root ball that his opponent had just thrown which unfortunately for Michael hit another rat giving Fester another point. The scores were even again.

Five-five, Michael thought. *There's all to play for, hit the last rat and I've won.* He swam to fetch the fallen ball but wasn't quick enough as Fester already had it in his scrawny paws. The disgusting creature went to play his dirty trick of hitting Michael in the face again but Michael was too clever this time and ducked under the water. The ball missed him. Luckily, he found the tangle of roots and got ready to knock the last rat and win the game. He took a moment, remaining very still. The boy watched Fester with stern eyes. *Revenge first*, he thought, tossing the ball as hard as his muscles would allow. The ball smashed into the rodent's slimy nose and its body plunged into the water like a sunken submarine. It felt like the ceiling of the cavern was going to crack and crumble from the noise of the watching rats—gnashing their teeth in anger at their fallen leader.

Michael swam towards Fester; not to see if he was alright but to get the ball. He found it without difficulty then pivoting neatly he slammed it into the last, hanging rat who howled in pain as it dropped limply to the canal rubbing its bottom.

"I've won, I've won!" yelled Michael. He was jumping up and down pumping his fist through the air. Evie was equally delighted. She rattled the cage and squawked like an agitated parrot.

"We did it Evie, we can go home." Michael beamed at his friend. The audience of rats had gone eerily quiet. They stood like sentinels, loyally waiting further orders. *Where was Fester?* Michael scanned the water until he saw an emerging lump of matted fur.

The lump ambled over to Michael who was now attempting to dry himself off with his tracksuit hoodie. "So, I won!" said Michael, proudly placing his cap back on his head.

"Not so fast!" wheezed Fester baring his front two teeth. "You broke the rules." Michael frowned and was about to speak but the rat went on, "You are unfortunately disqualified so that means I win." Michael furrowed his brow in disbelief.

"How am I disqualified? I played the game the same way as you."

"You hit me," whispered the rat," and it was a dangerous throw. You could have taken my eye out." Michael was now turning red.

"What?" he shouted. "What are you talking about, you hit me too."

"Ah, yes I did but my throw didn't cause you pain or damage. I threw the ball *safely* at you."

"That's ridiculous," yelled Michael indignantly. "Anytime someone throws something at someone else there's always potential to damage them. How is your throw different to mine? You hurt me, you know! I won fair and square so stop making excuses—give me back my dog and let Evie out of that cage. We're going home."

Fester turned his back to Michael and waved his white-tipped tail at him mockingly.

"I'm afraid that won't be happening," he snarled. The rat then swiped Michael's cap from his head and placed it on his own greasy scalp. "You see," he continued, "that deal we had—well I was never going to keep it. I don't know where your dog is. I sold her to some merchant. Oops, sorry but I lied." Michael stared at the creature in shock.

The rat nodded at the nearby rats, a gesture that meant 'lock him up'. Michael was furious. He launched himself at Fester, his hands out in front of him like two ferocious lobster claws and before the other rats could intervene he had knotted his hands around Fester's flabby neck. He applied pressure hoping to finish the horrible creature. Michael looked deeply into the rat's single eye. He was so angry he didn't care about hurting the rat. Seconds passed, Fester's eye bulged and his body grew limp. The other pyrats stood on their hind legs watching, in shock, not moving an inch, not making a sound. Michael was in control, he could end the life of this animal...but he didn't. Slowly he lifted his hands away leaving the rat gasping for breath. Michael had spared him. He couldn't do it, he couldn't kill this animal, however mean it had been.

Suddenly, as if someone had opened a window to the outside sun, Michael was enveloped in a golden light that seemed to radiate out from under his chin in fine tendrils. His body went rigid, tingling with heat. His eyes widened. He staggered with surprise, hardly breathing. The crowd of rats stared, dumbstruck. The light was so beautiful. The cavern was silent. Evie's mouth hung open in awe. *What was that light?* The glorious light spread out filling the dark space and hung there for a moment. As quickly as it had appeared, it vanished, leaving Michael standing alone, witless and confused. Evie wondered if she had actually witnessed this event or if she had just dreamt it. Light had just come out of Michael's chest—*that wasn't possible.* Michael too was lost in his own uncertainty. *What just happened to me? Did I die and turn into a spirit?*

Somewhere a rat broke the silence. Caught unawares, Michael quickly realised that he was not dead; in fact he was very much alive and was being overpowered by a fast-moving wave of foul rats. Without mercy, they crawled over him making him fall to the ground.

Chapter 11

The Canal Chase

The cavern was dark and cold. There wasn't a sound to be heard; all the rats were somewhere below, sleeping soundly. Fester had taken refuge further back in the cave. It had taken him some time to settle himself after his ordeal. Michael sat in his cage which hung next to Evie's. "I can hardly see a thing," she whispered. It was almost completely dark, the red eyes of the rats were all tightly shut during their sleep and only a scatter of glowing bugs crawled on a far wall. It was then that Michael remembered the luminobes in his tracksuit pocket. He took them out; they were motionless in his hand and were no longer glowing. They felt like a bunch of empty sweet wrappers—perhaps dead. He didn't like that he had caused these insects to die by having them hidden in his clothing all day. He gently rubbed the back of one of them and something wonderful happened; the beetle lit up like the bulb from a Christmas tree. So too did the others. Seeing the light, Evie rooted out her luminobes from her pocket as well. "Rub their backs," called Michael softly. She did as she was told and her insects glowed brightly too.

"Amazing," gasped Evie. "Now we can see each other." They took a moment to blink their way back to seeing clearly.

"Michael," said Evie after a minute, "what happened to you earlier, when you lit up? What was it? I have never seen that before?" Michael said nothing at first and then, "I dunno... I dunno what that was but it made me feel good about myself. Even though at that moment I hated the disgusting rat, I didn't want to kill him and I was calm in my choice. It was weird—kinda tricky to explain right now. Do you see?"

"I think so," said Evie in a hushed voice. She had her eyes lowered watching the beetles run through her open fingers. "How are we going to escape from here? We have to get out."

"You're right, we have to try and get out of here and search for Penny—there's still a chance we can find her." Michael pawed the bars and the lock of the cage with his free hand. "But how?" he murmured. "We're metres up, not to mention the fact that we have nothing useful to try and pick the lock with."

"Why did we listen to that glossum creature?" said Evie. "He led us towards danger. What are we going to do?" Michael had no answer to that. Escape seemed near impossible.

The children sat in their swinging prisons calmly trying to figure what to do when suddenly a whisper drifted up towards them.

"I may have led you to danger but I'm here now to help you escape, so I think you could say, one balances out the other." With puzzled looks, Evie and Michael shifted position in their cages and craned their necks to look down. They could just about make out the shape of Dvarku who was deftly scuttling up the wall of the cavern.

"I wanted to be here sooner so I must apologise about my tardiness but better late than never." The glossum was now next to Michael's cage and was gingerly gnawing at the lock with his super fine incisors. The lock popped and the cage door swung open, squeaking as it went.

"But why are you here… now… after sending us the wrong way... and into a trap?" asked Michael desperately. "No time for explanations. We need to move quickly and quietly; if we wake any one of those stinking pyrats below we're all for it——me included."

"They're called...pyrats?" asked Evie her brow ridged with lines.

"Yes, pyrats——they love to take things. They'll steal anything at any opportunity."

"The ugly one took my cap," said Michael.

"They're all ugly, Michael," said Evie without humour.

The glossum leaped up onto the roof of the cage and bit off a length of excess rope from near the pulley. "Here," it said, "secure this to the cage and use it to climb down. Be really careful not to step on a rat, the luminobes will show you the way." Michael looped the rope around one of the bars and pulled on it to test its strength. He placed a couple of luminobes on his forehead to act as a head torch and then started his descent. Dvarku had already given Evie some rope and was helping her tie it to the cage. She began to climb down too. Michael reached the floor of the cavern and cautiously tip-toed through the sleeping rats making his way to safe ground. Evie climbed down more slowly, her arms and legs getting weary.

"Go on," encouraged the glossum, "you're doing fine." Soon enough, she reached the stone floor looking triumphant.

Dvarku hopped over the bodies of the rats with ease towards Michael.

"This way," he whispered. Evie started to creep among the rats, almost holding her breath. She was nearly through the minefield of rodents when a pair of red eyes blinked randomly from the shadows under her nose. She got such a fright, she misjudged her careful footing and trod on several tails. *Rats*, she thought, *I've done it now*.

In no time at all, the rats woke up squealing and gnashing their teeth.

"Quickly!" shouted Dvarku, "around the corner there is an abandoned tangleraft, we can use it to escape. If we're lucky we can out sail them." It didn't take long for the rats to get on their feet and chase after the escapees.

The children and the glossum jumped onto the waiting raft. Dvarku bit through the mooring rope and then using his powerful tail, he propelled them through the water at high speed. A horde of angry rats scurried into view on the quayside. Dvarku drove the raft forward, faster still. The raft was made of tangleweed and soft clay. "Look! Two oars," he yelled at the children, "use them!" The captors were in the water now and on the move. The children began paddling faster, hoping to put some distance between them and the pyrats.

The canal was by no means straight; it went through a series of twists and turns and at each corner more rats appeared from all angles.

In between paddle strokes Michael looked down at the raft. It seemed to be made of the same roots that the ratsling ball was made from. Remembering how coarse and hard tangleweed was, Michael figured it would be perfect to throw and fend off the rats. He tried to rip some of it off but it was too tightly woven. Evie saw him and realised his thoughts.

"Here," she called to him, "what about this?" In her hands was sodden clay, prized from in between the roots. She had rolled some into a compact ball. "If you reach down through the roots there's plenty more. She glanced downwards at their feet. "Let's do it," she screamed wildly, flinging a clay ball at the approaching rats.

Just like she once told Michael, Evie had an excellent throw; the first ball landed in the middle of a pack of red eyes and must have sunk a quarter of the rats. Michael followed her lead and felt more confident with his aim and technique—especially after winning ratsling. They threw ball after ball of clay and between them, they put a stop to the swimming rats. The chase was done—no more rats were following. They applauded each other. "How resourceful of you Evie," said Dvarku with admiration, "I've never seen clay used like that. You two did an excellent job." He climbed aboard the raft and collapsed with exhaustion. The children continued paddling down the long tunnel, their hearts beating wildly with the past thrills of the day.

Meanwhile, Fester trampled about his den, seething at the escape of his captives.

"How could I let them go?" he screeched. Enraged, he reached up and whipped off Michael's cap. Looking at it with contempt, he tossed it into the canal where upon it drifted aimlessly away.

Chapter 12

Vilurbus

The raft floated down the canal. Evie and Michael had stopped rowing and were catching their breaths next to the glossum. The flow of water was a little faster here suggesting that the canal was heading to one central point. Other smaller waterways entered on the left and the right joining the main canal, all flowing in the one direction. The walls were lined with glowing torches of molten fire offering a welcoming light especially after the dank conditions of the rats' lair.

"Who put those torches there?" asked Evie, thumbing at a torch over her shoulder.

"Oh, that would be the dwellers," replied Dvarku nonchalantly.

"The who?" siad the children together.

"The dwellers—the people of Vilurbus."

"What's Vilurbus?" asked Evie. She had sat up abruptly, her curiosity stoked.

"Not what," said the glossum, "but rather your question should be 'where'. Vilurbus is our city, a wonderful place by all accounts, filled with culture and commerce and hard-working people. Well...most of them. I don't spend too much time there now but when I do, I always enjoy it. Except lately things have changed."

"How have things changed?" demanded Evie.

"I don't want to get into that right now. There will be explanations later."

Michael stood up and pulled at his earlobe. "Speaking of explanations," he said sternly, "you owe us a big one. Why did you send us straight into that awful rats' nest and then come and rescue us later. It doesn't make any sense. You also lied to me, you told me you knew where my dog Penny was."

"Michael, I am sorry for all that business but you see, I had to send you to Fester and his fiendish crew."

"You mean you meant for us to get caught?"

"Yes," replied Dvarku calmly. "I know how Fester behaves and I knew he would be a cheat, lie to you and then unfairly lock you up. I needed to see if you had any compassion, if you possessed a good heart." Michael shook his head, slightly confused by this information. "And Michael," the glossum continued, "here is the fantastic part—you do, you do have a heart, an honest heart. You spared that wretched animal's measly life. Even when you had a prime opportunity to end him and despite the beastly manner in which he treated you. You, my boy, are quite extraordinary."

"The light!" shouted Evie. "That gorgeous light that glowed from his chest. That must have something to do with this."

"Yes," answered Dvarku excitedly, "it does, the light blazed from his heart. You, Michael, are the answer to our prayers." With that, the glossum dived off the raft and dipped under the water.

"Wait!" called Michael. "What prayers? What do you mean? Tell me more about the light." Dvarku popped up and hung onto the raft with his wet paws. Water trickled down his face from his bent ears.

"Excuse me for a second, I just want to check if there's any clingfish stuck to the underside of our raft. It just dawned on me that I'm famished!"

"I'm famished too," said Evie patting her tummy. "Is there anything to eat down here?"

"Just roast rat, I guess" giggled Michael.

"Euugh!" said Evie. "No thanks, I'd rather do without than eat one of those nasty things."

Dvarku leaped back on board pulling a skinny, green fish after him. The fish looked like a deflated balloon with fins.

"There'll be food when we reach the city, don't worry, we won't starve you." He began to eat, then hesitated.

"Unless you want to share this?" Evie and Michael shook their heads slowly and sat down. "Never mind," spluttered the glossum," a sliver of fin flapping from his lower lip. The children watched on while he finished his meal then as if it were perfectly timed, he wiped his mouth with his paw and announced, "We're here. Welcome to Vilurbus."

The raft turned a corner and floated into a space the children could hardly believe existed. Their eyes were instantly drawn upwards to the broad ceiling. Immense stalactites studded with coloured crystals hung down majestically. Evie thought they looked like huge sparkly earrings. This cavern was so wide that you couldn't see the wall on the other side. In front of them was a curved marina dotted with little rafts just like theirs, and more elaborately-made boats. Behind the marina lay the city, a knot of streets and stone-carved buildings. In the centre of the city was a glass structure rising up like a cathedral, its point disappearing into the darkness. Down on the streets, people and animals hustled and bustled about.

"Wow," exclaimed Evie thoroughly impressed, "who on earth made this?"

"Well, not who," said the glossum, "but rather your question should be 'what'. And it's not on earth, it's under earth." The animal slapped his paws together gleefully at his own wit.

"This cave was made many, many years ago by water erosion. For the most part, the rock lying beneath Dublin is limestone and limestone can be worn away over time by the constant flow of water. All this water drips and flows downwards and gathers at this level—this canal or river that we're currently floating on."

"So all these caves and tunnels are made from many years of water erosion?"

"Exactly right," replied Dvarku. "Although this one was further eroded and refined by the first core masons who settled here long ago." Michael and Evie held blank expressions on their faces. Dvarku took the prompt.

"The core masons dug out this massive cave, constructed the buildings, designed the whole layout of the city."

The raft had finally stopped at the quayside and the glossum jumped off. He tied the raft to an empty metal ring that was laid in the rock with his useful teeth. Evie noted how dirty the quayside had become from the filthy water lapping up against it. The children clambered off, delighted to have something solid underfoot.

"Look Michael," cried Evie pointing excitedly at the ground. A string of the curious glowing frogs they had seen on the Liffey hopped and croaked merrily down the street. Upon seeing Michael they toddled over to him and crawled onto his trainers. Michael could feel their tingly heat and vibrations in his toes. The children giggled at their cheekiness.

"Are they still trying you tell you something?" said Evie.

"No time for merriment," said Dvarku noticing the growing throng of bystanders, "we need to get you some food. Let's go!" and with that he set off, marching through the busy streets towards one of the many inviting-looking taverns.

Chapter 13

The Merchant and his Wife

The tavern felt cosy and safe. In the centre was a fire pit filled with molten core rock. Core rock was mined deep within the earth—dangerous to extract but very, very long lasting. This piece was burning for six days already. The glossum and the children took a seat and within minutes a young girl no older than Evie brought them platters of food.

"I am so hungry," announced Evie. "I could eat anything!"

"Well that's good to hear, my dear because the food here is very different to what you're used to in Dublin, I'd wager." Dvarku pushed a hot, clay dish under her nose. The steam made its way up her nostrils.

"What is it?" she asked.

"Grilled bats' wings smothered in sticky boulic juice. The children looked at each other. They had never eaten bat before and what was boulic?

"Boulics are tubers, much like potatoes," explained Dvarku, "but with more juice. They grow deep in the earth." Michael and Evie eyed the food suspiciously, shrugged their shoulders and dug in.

Soon their fingers were dripping with sticky sauce and each had a pile of bat bones stacked neatly on their plate.

"Bat tastes just like chicken," they both agreed. In addition to this, there were black and white truffles baked in the oven, steamed river lettuce, a range of strange berries and some warm tea that was served in pewter cups and had the faintest aroma of ginger. The children ate their fill and their bellies thanked them for it.

With their appetites satisfied, Evie and Michael started to doze. They were rudely awakened with the entrance of a man who banged through the doors, his arms filled with small wooden crates.

"Hello Dvarku, how have you been?" he called piling the boxes next to the door.

"I'm very good. I've just had a delicious meal that I expect was prepared by your wife." The merchant smiled crookedly and turned towards the kitchen door and called, "Bronagh, I'm home, bring my pipe please."

Almost immediately a woman dressed in a grubby smock stepped through the kitchen door. Her chestnut hair framed her face; her fat cheeks were pink like an apple. In her hand was a stone ladle that she tapped against one of her round hips as she walked; in her other hand was the merchant's pipe. She kissed him on the forehead then lifted a small ember from the fire with a blackened tongs. As carefully as she could, she popped the glowing coal into the funnel of the pipe and handed it to her husband. Her face lit up when she noticed the children.

"Oh my, oh my," she twittered, plopping herself onto a chair, "landovers! Just look at you two, it's been years since we had landovers down here. I'm Bronagh and this is my husband Kerad. Pleased to meet you." The children reached over their hands and the two adults shook them; Bronagh warmly, Kerad half-heartedly.

"What are landovers?" said Evie.

"You know," replied Bronagh, her index finger pointing up towards the ceiling and everything else beyond, "you lot—people from above the ground. I've never been up there myself but I believe my mother was. She used tell me stories." *Landovers? They have words for everything and anything down here* thought Michael. Bronagh reached for the pot of ginger tea and refilled the children's cups.

"Why are they here?" said Kerad scratching his raggedy beard.

"They've lost their dog," said Dvarku, "but I really want them to meet the Librarian, it's most urgent." Despite the fact that not many animals have the ability to wink, Dvarku could manage it and he closed his left eye for more than two whole seconds grinning all the while and making sure both adults had caught his gesture.

"Oh my, oh my," giggled Bronagh, "are you sure Dvarku?" She clapped her hands with excitement. Kerad watched on saying nothing, his pipe puffing away like a sleeping dragon.

"Which one?" he then asked suddenly, "the boy or the girl?"

"The boy," replied Dvarku. The children listened closely, trying to deduce what was going on. *What were they talking about*, wondered Michael. It was about him, he was sure of that. And it must be something to do with the light that came out of him...but what exactly. The adults continued to talk as if the children weren't even there. Suddenly, Michael cracked, he couldn't take their talking in riddles any longer.

"Stop it. Stop it. I don't know what you're talking about." He had raised his hands up in an action of desperation and was staring at the faces around the table. "You're not making any real sense. I *am* clever enough to know that you're talking about me so please let me in on the big secret. If I'm so important, surely I should at least know *why* I'm so important." Nothing.

Dvarku bounded up onto the table and spat out a gold nugget from his mouth as payment for the food. He then made his way to the door.

"Where are you going?" shouted Evie across the empty tavern, "Michael just asked you a question, and an important one at that." The glossum bowed politely, his head almost touching the floor tiles.

"Follow me," he said, "and I'll introduce you to someone who will explain everything."

Chapter 14

The Librarian

The glossum darted through the city, scurrying and squirming left and right, through and around the legs of the city dwellers. At one point it seemed like he was about to chase his own tail. The others followed his path. Kerad and Bronagh were grinning, clearly amused at his excitement. Michael dragged his feet along the busy street, a little unsure of whether meeting somebody else was going to help in his quest to find Penny.

Before long they crossed a wide, public square which was marked by lines of burning lanterns. At one corner stood the great building that looked like it had been cut from glass. You could just make out shapes and shadows from within which flickered and seemed to change colour in the light of the lanterns.

Dvarku jumped onto his hind legs and leaned forward pushing on a section of the building. A large hunk of glass slid neatly aside to reveal a doorway. Michael looked up upon entering the building and noticed a logo cut into the wall. It showed three books surrounded by a thin, red circle. All the books were open, their pages flapping—briefly displaying all the knowledge that lay within.

The smell inside was similar to that of any library in the world; a smell of paper; dry and musty— lovingly crafted using metallic-scented ink and printed with pride by the hands of people long ago—a scent of history, of intrigue, of friendship and of course knowledge. There was minimal furniture in the room— a small table and a couple of chairs. Every available space was fitted with stone-carved shelving that heaved with books. Even the floor was made of books, tightly stacked together like tiles. The children walked timidly on the carpet of coloured leather-bound pages and stopped in the middle of the room where a tall, bony man sat clasping his hands together. He held an expression that was neither hostile nor friendly. He pushed a pair of wooden spectacles onto his bald head and creased his fuzzy eyebrows so that they met in the middle above his nose. His ears were elf-like, coming to a point at one end, his skin dark and shiny. He twitched his chin as if he were chewing grass like a hungry cow.

The party stood around him in a loose circle. Michael wondered whether he should say something and was just about to open his mouth but then paused. He spied something moving on the table behind the man. It was not one, not two, but three of the same, remarkable frogs that had teased him when he was on the trip up the Liffey; the same band of frogs that had retreated through the hole in the wall—these frogs were pretty common down here it seemed. Michael remembered the first place he had encountered one of these frogs; at home in his back garden with Penny by his side. The dog's image flashed in his mind and he reminded himself that right now, he must do all he can to locate her. He decided he would hear this guy out, that maybe he could help find Penny. Michael was pretty keen to get out of this underground place—the sooner he found his dog, the sooner he could go home. His daydream was smashed with the sound of a voice that echoed throughout the glass structure.

"Welcome to the Coreland and welcome to the Library." The man they called the Librarian walked towards Michael and placed both his hands on the boy's shoulders. "It is wonderful to have you landovers come and visit us and you, I'm informed, are quite special." He pointed a bony finger directly at Michael, an expectant stare in his eyes.

"Look," said Michael calmly. "Before you waste your time explaining why you think I'm special, don't bother. All I'm interested in is finding my dog and going home." Dvarku jumped onto the Librarian's shoulders and faced Michael.

"Please keep an open mind and listen to the Librarian...please." Michael was getting fed up of listening.

"I'm not interested, I want to leave here—right now with my dog. I don't trust you or anyone else."

"Michael, I know I told you I knew where your dog was and then lied to you," whispered the glossum, "but if it weren't for me, you'd be lying at the bottom of a slumber pool, dead, or worse again, hanging in a cage as a prisoner of Fester. Please, oh please listen to the Librarian without interruptions and then afterwards we can talk about Penny. Please!" The animal pleaded with Michael, its paws pressed together tightly.

"Alright then," said Michael. For a split second, it sounded like the Library, as well as the dwellers let out a sigh of gratitude.

A hush fell over the room as the Librarian began to speak again, his tone serious and straightforward. "Michael," he began, "we need your help. Our water supply is poisoned. It is dirty beyond compare. The wildlife found in the canals and waterways is dying...and so too are the people." Evie recalled the pathetic clingfish Dvarku was feeding on. "Our core masons have tried digging for another water source but there isn't one. The waterway network is a single system in these parts and once one area becomes spoilt, so too does everywhere else." *That explained the filthy water everywhere* Michael figured. "We are able to purify the water we have by boiling it but it is getting dirtier by the day and soon no amount of boiling will make it drinkable. In short, we are all heading for mass dehydration. All the dwellers in this city will die and soon after that all the creatures too."

"What's causing this water situation?" asked Michael, remembering the news report he saw on TV. "There are problems with the water in Dublin too. Are they linked, do you think?" Bronagh's pink face changed to white. Kerad had taken his pipe from his pocket and was nervously twisting it in his fists.

"We have a reason for this terrible problem," began the Librarian again. "It's because of the Mayoress— a selfish woman of no virtue. She takes the good out of everything for her own gain and enjoys seeing others less fortunate than her suffer. She is ruining the water and it seems she is responsible for the lack of water in Dublin as well. She is more than likely using some means of trickery to drain it all away from your city, drip by drip."

Michael went to pull the peak of his cap down over his eyes and then realised that it was stolen by Fester. Instead he scratched his head. What should he do? *Should I help them* he wondered *even though I'm unsure how I can. What about Penny? I don't want her to die down here, alone. Where is she?*

"I'll stay until I find my dog. Then I'm leaving," he announced. "I'm sorry, I don't think I can help you." The Librarian cast his eyes to the floor. Dvarku shook his head, his usually upright ears hanging limp at this neck. Evie turned to face Michael, her eyes wide. Michael recognised the same look when she first agreed to help him find Penny.

"Really Michael?" she said softly, "we're going to leave them without trying?" Michael exhaled. Evie was right—they needed to stay. He turned to the Librarian.

"How can we help you?" he asked. The man smiled, his white teeth bold against his black lips.

"We think you, my boy, have the gift," explained the Librarian.

"The light?" said both children at the same time. "Yes the light. If what Dvarku tells me about you is true, then you are the only one who can defeat her."

"But what can *I* do. Why do you need me? You have enough people here to overthrow her—put *her* in a cage."

"She would love to possess the gift—using it to wield dark magic and do wrong but luckily for us she doesn't. She is however a master elixir mixer and can cook up poisons, potions and nasty spells with great skill. The

Mayoress is the creator of the hideous slumber pools that we have down here." Evie frowned.

"But why would she make the slumber pools, "she asked. "What does she gain from them?"

"Just to laugh at those who fall in and die." replied Bronagh solemnly. Sensing the children's uneasiness, Bronagh continued with more hopeful news, "Michael, we believe you have the gift. It can be so powerful. It is possible that you can do this."

"What exactly is the gift?" asked Evie.

"It can be the most wonderful thing. It can do good things." The Librarian thrust his hands in his pockets and walked around the table. One of the three frogs was asleep, another sitting quietly on its head. The third remained still, listening closely. "The earth is a sphere and is made up of several layers," said the Librarian waving his hands about. "The very centre is called the core, a fiery place of vast energy burning constantly. Our brave core masons delve to places near the core and extract molten core rock which we use for light and heat. The core gives off waves of special energy that only a few people and creatures are affected by. These firemoths above us are one of those creatures; they give off their core energy in the form of light." Everyone's eyes were drawn to the glowing moths that were gently buzzing about the glass ceiling. Evie recognised these moths as the insects they had seen in the tunnels earlier that day.

"What about luminobes?" asked Michael. The Librarian pushed his spectacles further up on his head and continued, "Yes, luminobes are another example of a creature who emits core energy. "

"Don't forget me!" called Dvarku waving his tail until it shimmered.

"Those examples are insects and animals," said Michael, "what about people?" The Librarian stooped down and picked up a book that lay in a section of the floor. It was a fat book, bound in a soft, brown material quite like animal skin. Down the spine were silver letters displaying something Evie and Michael couldn't make out. The Librarian let it fall onto the table with a thud causing the yellow pages to flutter. Evie brushed her hand along its edge.

"What is it?" she asked.

"'The Archives of Agon'," announced the Librarian with pride. "Everything we know about core energy is recorded in here." He leafed through the dusty book and then presented a page to Michael and Evie pointing at the title.

Core Energy Personality Qualities

Positive

The recipient of true core energy can glean their power by means of the following favourable traits: thoughtfulness, helpfulness, kindness, selflessness, friendliness and meekness.

Negative

It is rather rare and unwelcome but it is possible for an individual to be gifted in magic and power derived from unfavourable traits. These include: selfishness, deceit, spite, laziness and wrath.

The children finished reading and stood there in silence, processing the details. Their thoughts were promptly interrupted.

Outside there was a chatter of voices. Shadows darkened the glass walls of the library. It seemed a crowd was gathering in the square. Evie swept her fingers through her fringe, contemplating a question, "So, what positive character trait did Michael have when the light shone from him?"

"Well," answered the Librarian walking around the table, his hands flapping madly, "you must think about what he did at the time, was he kind, friendly, selfless or was it a mixture of several of these qualities? In some cases the individual can possess lots of the traits and as such, is much more powerful." Michael said nothing. He was feeling overwhelmed by this information—core energy— picked up by him and then let shine from him whenever he was friendly or maybe kind— it seemed bizarre and yet he couldn't deny those mysterious beams and how he felt letting that rat live. *This is all too weird,* he thought, *I can't stay here. I'm no hero. I want to go home.*

The Librarian had seated himself and was now polishing his spectacles with the end of his shirt. The three frogs were lounging contentedly on the table. Michael was about to tell the Librarian his plans to leave when one of the frogs lit up and began to vibrate softly.

"I'm Parabisis," it said in its strange, ringing voice. This is Sondos here asleep beside me and up there is Koax." Parabisis threw its eyes up to the frog who was neatly sitting upon the head of Sondos, the sleeping frog. "I believe you have an amazing power and that you can help us. You may be the only hope we have. You have the gift. Please say you'll do it. Please help us." Michael considered the request for a heartbeat then shook his head sadly. "I'm sorry; I'm not the one for you. I need to go home.'

Chapter 15

Drought in Dublin

Dublin city was burning. The summer delivered warm, sunny days with very little rain. The temperatures were in the high twenties and it was hot. The city council had to halt the flow of water to limit its use. The inhabitants wanted to drink even more water, take extra cold showers and keep their taps running more than they normally would, but they couldn't—the city had a water shortage to begin with and this problem was only made worse by the wonderfully, warm weather.

Everyone was finding the drought and the heat tough: local farmers in nearby suburban market gardens had to watch while their strawberries ripened all too quickly and then rotted before their eyes turning into a messy, red mush, the elderly were advised to stay indoors, seated in the shade with damp towels draped around their necks, in local universities water polo teams were left high and dry with a near-empty pool to practise in, even the ducks felt the changes—in St. Stephen's Green, the mallards and moor hens had no option but to lounge lazily in oozy mud instead of floating about in cooling water.

Hydrologists were flummoxed as to where the water had gone; the water levels in rivers had dropped and several lakes had just dried up completely. Although the weather was warm and there was a lot of evaporation, it still didn't make any sense, there should be much, much more water available at this time of the year— *where was all the water, it must have gone somewhere?*

Joan Devoy sat at her kitchen table with her head in her hands. Her brow was furrowed with worry and her eyes looked empty. She didn't care about the heat or the lack of water—her son was missing. Across the table sat Evie's parents who were also at their wits' end. *Where were the children* they all wondered? A little while ago, they had been questioned by two burly Gardaí who were doing their best to get valuable information on the whereabouts of the children. The two men had also spent the afternoon at the school where they interviewed Miss Meehan and Mr Sykes; anyone who was associated with the children was asked questions to see if they could provide anything useful.

With nothing else to be done that day, Evie's parents wished Joan well and went home. The day gave no leads and no useful information. Joan was no closer to finding her son who had now been missing for 24 hours.

Realising that she had hardly eaten all day, she switched the kettle on to make a cup of tea and popped some bread in the toaster. There was a knock. Joan opened the door to find the lanky figure of Dmitri waiting there. He thrust his hand out awkwardly for her to shake it.

"Hi Mrs Devoy, I'm Dmitri, I'm in school with Michael and Evie. I haven't met you properly."

"Oh yes...Dmitri, I believe you were questioned at the school earlier. Do you know anything that would help?"

"I told them all I know, which wasn't much." Dmitri stepped from one foot to the other in an uneasy shuffle. "I've spent the last few weeks with Michael and Evie in summer school and now summer camp. I hope they're found."

"So do I, dear." With her eyes lowered she started to shut the door. "Good night dear," she said.

"I felt we patched things up," blurted Dmitri. "We had had a few fights, Michael and I, but I think we had made things better between us. That day on the river—we had started talking to each other again —Evie was there too. The two of them were getting on really well. Michael was taking photos of her and everything was great. I don't think they ran away." Dmitri stopped talking and gulped involuntarily. For an instant Mrs Devoy looked past him, lost in her own thoughts. "Mrs Devoy," he repeated, "I don't think he ran away."

"Photos," she murmured. "His camera is gone. Wherever he has got to, he must have taken his camera with him." She smiled weakly. "Sorry dear, I'm just thinking out loud. I guess I should mention that to the investigating Garda. Well, I'm glad to hear you and Michael had stopped bickering." She nodded at him, said good night and shut the door. Dmitri turned from the front door, zipped up his jacket and set off for home.

Chapter 16

Mikey Heartblaze

Michael was sticking to his decision. Enough was enough. As much as it hurt him to admit, he needed to give up the search for Penny and get himself home. Goodness knows how is mother was feeling, she would be worried sick. He turned and walked from the library.

"You coming Evie?" he called, "let's go home." Evie felt the need to say goodbye to their new friends but she could see Michael didn't so she just waved hurriedly and followed him out the door.

Outside, the square was loaded with hundreds of people, their chattering filling the air. When Evie and Michael appeared from the library, a soft hush spread through the crowd like spilt honey sliding along a floor. The children gazed out at the sea of faces not sure what they should do. The silence ended abruptly with a cry from the crowd.

"Is it true? Are you the one?" Michael looked around him; he was uncertain what to answer. The sound of voices rose again. Michael said nothing. Thankfully the Librarian, complete with frogs on his shoulder walked up beside the boy.

"We believe he is," said the Librarian signalling the crowd to be quiet with his large hands.

"And what proof have you got?" The voice had now become clearer and louder. The Librarian stood on his toes trying to identify the speaker.

"The boy was confirmed in possessing core energy in the west tunnel by Dvarku earlier today."

"You're relying on second-hand information from a glossum! I thought you would have requested confirmation from a more reliable source, Malachi. You should be more careful as to what you believe."

"I believe that glossums never lie." Michael suddenly recalled when Dvarku sent him the wrong way to the rats' lair and he smiled for the glossum had explained the necessity of that stunt—to see if Michael possessed a good heart.

"But you didn't see it for yourself?" the voice pressed Malachi some more.

"Sometimes *not* seeing is the best way to believe in something. You must have faith, in everything, no matter what."

"I, for one," said the voice again, "am not willing to believe that this boy is the answer to our problems." The owner of the voice had finally made his way to the front of the crowd and was pointing straight at Michael. The fat, rough head of the man resembled a boulder which was kind of amusing because he was a core mason whose job was to dig through rock. He was not happy and the more he ranted, the more other voices began to echo the same sentiment.

"Please, everyone try not to get upset. Time will tell if this boy has the gift," called the Librarian, his voice lifting above the heads of the people and drifting to the far reaches of the square. "Is there anyone else who would like to speak?"

A thin woman by the name of Marta pushed her way through the front line of people and stopped before Michael, Evie and the Librarian. In her arms was a tiny girl with her face buried in her mother's neck. The woman put the child down and resting her hands protectively on the girl's head, looked at the Librarian squarely in the face.

"We have had enough. There is no clean water and food supplies are getting dangerously low. This is Tella, my daughter. Her eyes have been poisoned—she fell into some of the foul water and now she had been robbed of her sight." She reached down and embraced the child. The Librarian looked horrified. "We need a plan of action to defeat the Mayoress. She is evil and must be stopped." There was a murmur of agreement in the crowd. The woman continued, "Don't insult us by presenting us with a boy who *may* have special powers. We don't know anything about him. *He* could be on her side for all we know." The woman half turned around to the crowd to make her point. "Instead, tell us that there is a plan put in place and have us rally together to finish this senseless pollution of our water. Let us work together and defeat the Mayoress once and for all."

The crowd cheered, applauding the woman's brave words. Evie grabbed Michael's hand and moved closer to his side. They briefly looked at each other feeling uncomfortable with being at the centre of this water crisis. Evie was unsure what next to do so she knelt down and brushed the hair from the blind girl's bloodshot eyes—an act of kindness. Suddenly, the girl screamed—a scream that would wake the dead. Evie sprung up from the ground holding her hands up.

"I...I... didn't do anything to her," she stammered, "I didn't even speak to her." The girl was patting the ground around her frantically—searching. Her mother lifted her into her arms trying to comfort her.

"My dog, my dog—where's Lulu? Where is she?" Through gasps of air the girl called for her lost dog. The crowd stared at the child, her face awash with salty tears. *Did she even have a dog with her? There was no dog here. What was she talking about?*

Then suddenly a distant bark boomed through the crowded square. Michael was in no doubt—it was Penny. He began calling her name excitedly.

"Penny, Penny." The little girl showed relief on her face as she too recognised the bark.

"Oh Lulu," she shouted, her arms reaching out in front of her, "you've come back!"

Penny bounded in out of nowhere and leapt at Michael. He managed to catch her in his arms. She licked his face lovingly; she was delighted to have her old pal back again. The crowd moved back a little and observed this caring union between a boy and his dog.

"Penny, thank goodness you're back girl. I've been looking for you everywhere. We're going to go home." Michael stroked the dog's head and hugged her tightly.

The blind girl reached out and found the dangling tail of Penny. She tugged on it while gently whispering the word 'Lulu' over and over. Penny clambered out of her master's arms, found the girl and nuzzled her under her chin. The little girl's tears dried up and her face was now creased with the biggest smile you've ever seen.

"Lulu," she muttered, "don't ever run off on me again like that. I thought you were right beside me. Remember Lulu, I can't see too well now that my eyes are poisoned. I was frightened but then I found you and now you help me when I'm lost—Lulu, you are my lucky star."

Evie exchanged a glance with Michael and bent down to the little girl and in her most caring voice said, "Tella, we have been looking for this dog. She belongs to my friend Michael. We've come to take her back with us. We're really sorry."

The child threw her arms around the furry neck of the dog almost crushing her.

"No, please," she wailed, "don't take her. I need her, I love her." With these words, a ghostly silence fell upon the crowd. They stood, watching, waiting. *What would the boy's response be?* A single bat flew over the heads of the watching dwellers, its wings flapping in a steady beat. Michael knelt down beside Evie and tapped Penny on the head. He scratched her ears playfully. He then leaned over and whispered in the child's tiny ear. Another bat flew overhead. The girl's face was blank, almost pale and lifeless. She reached around looking for her mother's hands. Seconds later, the child began to cry again.

Michael rose from the ground and turned away. The crowd remained silent.

"Thank you, thank you, thank you," sobbed the young girl, her voice barely audible.

"What's happening?" called several voices standing nearby. Evie guessed what had happened;

Michael had just allowed the girl to keep Penny since the dog brought her such joy. To the sound of quiet gasps of disbelief from the bystanders, a brilliant bolt of light shot out of Michael's chest right from his beating heart. The gleaming bolt extended to the young girl and then refracted off her head and shone above and around the city of Vilurbus as an unmade jigsaw of a thousand pieces of light. The whole city became as bright as the sun and the crowd instinctively used their hands to cover their eyes.

What followed was amazing; the frogs' strange sounds rang out clear and melodic in a song of celebration that hummed and buzzed and seemed to blend with the fragments of golden light that danced above. The crowd gasped at the spectacle; they were truly awestruck, most of them had never seen anything like this. The light and the sound seemed to meander around each other forming an exciting circus for the senses. The dwellers were so captivated by what they saw that began to chant a name—low and soft at first but then growing in volume—over and over they chanted, getting louder with every second until their own voices became one single, chthonic noise—a heavy, booming roar that reminded Michael of the sound of a big, bass drum. 'Heartblazer...Heartblazer...Heartblazer'.

The Librarian pushed his glasses onto his shiny head and smiled. Kerad and Bronagh grabbed each other's hands tightly. The glossum couldn't contain himself; he raced around, his ears pointing up.

"He has the power, he is the one!" called the Librarian to the throng. The crowd continued to chant and scream and shout such was their excitement. It was just then that Marta, the girl's mother, lifted the girl into her arms and realised what had actually taken place; the light that shone out of Michael's chest had healed her daughter's eyes, returning her sight to her. The woman was overcome with joy. She embraced Michael fiercely, thanking him again and again for what he had done.

Now the people of Vilurbus knew that this boy, this landover, did possess the ability, through honourable magic to defeat the Mayoress and her motley crew of pyrats. This boy could save the water for all dwellers and animals alike.

The Librarian placed his hands on Michael's shoulders once more, his look was solemn, his ebony eyes full of anticipation.

"Will you help us?" he whispered. Michael answered more sure than he ever was before.

"Yes," he replied. "I will."

Chapter 17

The Cleansing Elixir

"Wow!" exclaimed Evie. "I don't know what to say. I'm lost for words."

"Me too," said Michael. They were sitting next to a roaring fire in the library—Malachi insisted they take a moment alone from all the excitement.

"The light that shone from you," said Evie, "how did you do that? It was more amazing this time than when it happened in the rats' lair...and you healed a girl from blindness. You have the power to heal—that's incredible!" Michael lifted his head from the rug and shrugged, his face weary. "Do you really want to give up Penny?" asked Evie suddenly, her expression turning stern, "are you sure about helping these people? We could say goodbye to all this and just make our way home." Evie paused a moment letting the shadows from the fire dance across her hands, then continued, "We have Penny now, Michael. We have what we came for. We should get home. Our parents must be so worried about us." Overwhelmed by Evie's questioning, Michael sighed.

"I can't," he said softly. "I feel I've got to help them. I have a gift. If I don't help them what have they got left?"

"But what about your mother; she probably thinks you're dead. We need to go home. There must be someone other than you down here who has similar powers and could help."

"There doesn't seem to be. If there is, why haven't they already tried to fix the problem?"

"Maybe they've all given up," said Evie tidying her messy hair.

"I can do this Evie. It's not impossible."

"I'm not so sure," she muttered. "Aren't you worried about this Mayoress person? She could be dangerous." Michael's temples throbbed. This decision was tough for him to make—it was tiring him out. Every time Evie opened her mouth, he had second thoughts. He must make up his mind.

"Evie, I want to stay and help. I feel good about this. Since my dad left me I haven't been happy but here I feel happy. I know I can make a difference and that makes me feel good about myself. We should do this Evie."

"And what about our parents?"

"We'll be quick enough. We'll be back home in no time. When will we ever get this opportunity again?" Evie twisted a lock of hair around her index finger and stared blankly into the fire.

"Okay," she agreed, "let's do it. Let's make a difference."

Just then the Librarian entered the building in a flurry.

"Lots to do," he called, "lots to do."

"When can we put a plan in action?" asked Michael brightly.

"We must move at once," replied the librarian. "You'll need some extra help—a team to aid you in your quest if you will." He chuckled lightly. "And a little something extra." He spun around, his coat flying behind him like a dull-looking flag and opened the 'Archives of Agon' for the second time that day. The pages of the heavy book flapped through his fingers sending a waft of silver-laden dust up into the air. The children looked on, puzzled. "Fragments of quartz," declared the Librarian coughing.

Searching quietly, his fingers poised over a long list of words, the Librarian was lost in thought. Evie's eyes moved to his pockets. Something was moving inside. *What under earth could that be* she wondered. To her relief, it was the three frogs. The Librarian scooped them out one by one and placed them on the table. Koax was still sitting awkwardly on the head of the sleeping Sondos, one of his amphibian feet stuck in the other frog's shut eye. Parabisis was fully alert and seemed to be the spokesperson for the trio.

"Mikey Heartblaze," it croaked, "I'm so glad you're staying to help us, I secretly knew you would. I had a feeling you might be a Heartblazer but I needed you to realise for yourself." It blinked twice making its eyes bulge, then directed its voice at the Librarian. "Malachi, are we going to mix up some potions?"

"I'm already looking into it," replied the Librarian still examining the ancient book. "Aha, here it is!" he announced. "On this mission, we need to try and clean the water and this cleansing elixir should do the trick."

"Is this a book of spells?" asked Evie.

"Not so much spells but rather ideas," replied Malachi. "Ideas and recipes to create magic however, they can only be obtained by using core energy which your friend Mikey has shown he can produce."

Michael leaned over the book trying to read about the elixir.

"How does it work?" he asked.

"An elixir is a potion," croaked Parabisis. "A mixture of different plants and animal parts and other things that you find in the Coreland. Their potency is activated when you add some core energy. We're going to make an elixir that will purify the filthy water. This will be the first step in our mission to solve the Coreland's problem."

From a bench at the back of the library, Malachi was spottering about; searching and grabbing with his large hands. He reappeared clutching an assortment of stone jars and bottles and stumbled back to the children, placing the items next to the book. Evie inspected the contents of the jars.

"Oo," she shrieked pinching the end of her nose. "What's so stinky?" The sludge in the jar was a revolting, green colour.

"That would be tangleroot that's been soaked in rats' breath—sometimes the foulest things can do the most good," muttered the Librarian setting out bowls, spoons and a large cleaver made of stone.

Parabisis jumped onto the open page of the book and started to call out the ingredients of the recipe while Malachi mixed them.

"To the rats' breath, add a handful of cinnamon clay, two pinches of red salt, a cupful of sand, a single bat's foot and seven flambiggle leaves." The Librarian worked quickly. The resulting paste looked quite horrid. "It looks awful, I know," said the Librarian but when we add some of Mikey's core energy it will become something wonderful." Everyone looked at Michael expectantly. He stared back with saucer-shaped eyes. "What?" he said. "I don't know how to make the light shine… it just happens!" The Librarian scratched his cheek and lifted his shades from his nose.

"Mmh," he said, "I had a feeling this might be the case. There is no true way to teach you how to command your powers—it is something you must learn on your own and you will learn—in time." Michael suddenly looked serious. He didn't like the feeling of uncertainty. This was something completely new to him, something that might take forever to understand. When he was learning to swim it took a long time with plenty of practice and plenty of mistakes. He needed to learn how to control this core energy quickly—the sooner, the better and what's more, he couldn't afford to make any mistakes.

Noticing his sudden change of mood, the Librarian pulled up a chair and sat beside the boy.

"Mikey, never lose faith in yourself and what you can achieve. Always take a challenge seriously, showing dedication and above all passion—passion is the key. Someone once said that if you're passionate about something, you should let that passion burn and if you do, who knows the wonders you can achieve—why you could set the world on fire."

"Who said that?"

"I did." The Librarian chuckled gleefully. Michael, beginning to feel better laughed with the jolly man.

"What else could Michael learn from the Archives of Agon?" inquired Evie.

"Well, plenty," replied Parabisis, "but for the moment, we should just try and create this cleansing elixir. There will, I'm sure, be another time for learning new things."

"What if Michael doesn't manage to make his heart glow again?" asked Evie her voice full of concern. Malachi ignored the question. Parabisis closed his eyes as if asleep.

The question remained unanswered. The silence was slashed with the opening of the glass door. In marched Kerad followed by two others.

"Here are the volunteers," he announced.

"Oh, good," said Malachi approaching them, "you've gathered a team together for this mission." He looked around, confused. "But where are the others?"

"This is it, Malachi, no one wants to risk their life chasing that woman," said Kerad, "she is greatly feared." Malachi shook his head sadly.

"It will have to do."

Michael studied the trio; there was Kerad who he'd already met, stern-faced, standing straight as a poker, his pipe in his hand. Beside him were two boys about Michael's age. The first was called Essop. His thick frown made him look like he was sitting the hardest exam ever and he wasn't doing very well at it. He stared intensely at Michael, his eyes not leaving the other boy's face. Michael was starting to feel uneasy at this behaviour but then Essop started to laugh lightly.

"Hi!" he said cheerfully, pulling his long locks from around his ears and letting them fall across his frown lines. "I was only pretending to be super serious just like Kerad 'cause I thought that's what type of man was needed for this mission." He nudged Kerad in the ribs. The older man hardly moved.

The team stood to attention without making a murmur. It seemed that everyone was waiting for Mikey to speak. Mikey shoved his hands in his pockets and coughed once.

"Well, thanks for joining me. And humour is always good Essop. Thanks." Further silence. Mikey bit his lip. *Come on*, he thought, *you can do better than that. At least pretend that you have a plan. They're all relying on you. At least pretend that you believe in yourself.* He removed his hands from his pockets and stood up a little straighter, his voice and his body more confident.

"However," he continued," we still want to get the job done properly so I need to know you're all going to do your best and help me." Essop raised his chin and nodded frantically.

"Yes, yes Mikey, you can count on us."

"Glad to hear it," said the Librarian. "This mission is a pretty big deal." Mikey glanced at Kerad for some sign of agreement. Kerad noticed him looking and shifted his weight from one leg to the other.

"I'll be there to help out any way I can," he grunted. "That is," he continued, "until I think that a particular plan is not the best course of action, then I will do my own thing." Mikey nodded curtly and then turned to the second boy.

"What about you?" he asked. It was as if everyone in the room had forgotten the other boy's existence; he was so pale and slight, so insignificant, standing on his spindly legs with his slender arms wrapped around his torso. He was motionless, silent——even his clothes didn't rustle. He had his head bent under a thick velvet-like cap, his eyes fixed on the book-lined floor.

"My name is Lodie," he said meekly.

"Do you think you'll be able for this challenge?" asked Michael right next to the boy's face causing him to raise his head and look Michael in the eye.

"I will, surely. I will do my very best to defeat the Mayoress."

"I'm glad to hear it because we're going to need all the help we can get." Mikey studied all the faces around him. They were bright with anticipation, full of positivity. The same could not be said for him; he was putting on a brave face. Inside, he was panicking. The dwellers truly believed in him and he wasn't about to let them down even if he was uncertain about what to do. He didn't know how to make his powers just appear and he needed to conjure some core energy from his heart in order to activate the elixir. He couldn't back out now, he promised to help these people. He would take a risk he decided and hope for the best.

He was brought back to the weighty reality of the situation by Evie who was clicking her fingers in his face.

"Mikey, Mikey!" she called softly. Her face had a puzzled look to it, her eyes half-closed with tiredness. Mikey gazed past her—lost somewhere.

"Are you alright?" asked Kerad, "you look dazed. We've been calling you for a while now."

"I was just daydreaming," answered Mikey. They chuckled at him. *This boy whom the city dwellers were relying on to defeat the Mayoress and bring clean water to all...was a daydreamer!*

"Leave him be," said the Librarian, "he's just getting his head together. I bet he's a little awestruck. Let him dream. Daydreamers are lucky; they practise using their imaginations twice as much as the rest of us. Morning and night!"

"Did you just have an awesome idea?" asked Evie her eyes suddenly bright again, "an awesome plan for this mission?"

"What? Eh, yeah! I did. I mean, I do," lied Michael, gulping down a thick lump of uncertainty.

Chapter 18

Evie Takes a Stand

The city was fizzing with excitement; there were boats and rafts bobbing across the marina filled with onlookers—each desperately trying to see the children. More had assembled on the quay; all clambering to get a look at the team of brave guardians setting out to right all the wrongs generated by the Mayoress. There was whistling and cheering from the crowd. Mikey looked around him, astounded. Hands were waving, mouths smiling. *It's the boy*, they shouted to each other, *the Heartblazer. He and his team are going to help us.* Evie and Mikey were still a little shook by how much everyone was depending on them.

Mikey helped Lodie and Essop haul supplies onto the waiting boats while Kerad inspected the mooring ropes making sure they were in sound condition. The boats were stocked with small supplies of fresh water, a lantern of firemoths to show the way, some catapults made from tangleweed and bats' wings, a medical bag of ointments and bandages and a curious looking compass which had markings for 'core' and 'away from core' instead of markings for north and south.

"Here you go Mikey," said Malachi shoving a small, glass bottle in Michael's tracksuit pocket and zipping it securely. "It's the cleansing elixir. I've put it in a glass bottle so the light can penetrate it. When you summon your core energy, just place the bottle in the rays of light and this will activate the mixture." Mikey nodded patting his pocket.

With the boats ready, they began to board. Evie stepped on the first boat and settled herself at the rear. Kerad who was busy untying the second boat from the quayside called to her, "what are you doing? You cannot come with us." Evie had to check to make sure he was addressing her.

"What do you mean?" she said forcefully. "Of course I'm coming." The people at the quayside went very quiet. All eyes were on Evie. "I'm not going to stay here," she continued, "I want to help." Malachi stepped out from the crowd and squatted down beside Evie. He took her hand in his and smiled reassuringly.

"Women in the Coreland never go on a mission such as this; women don't mine, they don't fish and they certainly don't fight against someone as dangerous as the Mayoress. You can stay here." Evie blinked at the old man in disbelief then threw her head back in an amazing fit of laughter. She could just manage to speak in between her loud guffaws.

"I've never heard such rubbish," she shrieked, her face pink and puffy. "Women are as capable as men in completing a mission; mining or fishing or building or winning a competition or whatever successes you may think of. I am *not* staying here and you can't make me."

"But you must," pleaded Malachi. Kerad nodded his agreement as did all the men standing nearby. Evie was no longer laughing now. Her face was no longer pink. She looked ghostly pale, her lips thin, her eyes narrowed. She gestured to the crowd in a long, dramatic sweep.

"Do all the women here agree with the men? That they should stay put and not have the choice in where they go or what they do? That only men should be allowed to do the important, dangerous jobs?" She paused, waiting for a response. No one answered her. Michael approached the boat cautiously.

"Are you okay?" he asked. "Don't get upset."

"I'm going with you," she replied sitting back further in the seat and folding her arms. "And I dare any other woman to come as well." She suddenly stood up careful not to topple the boat and yelled at the women in the crowd. "Don't let the men bully you. You should be all equal in everything you do." The crowd was now eerily silent. In fact, it was so quiet you could have heard a glossum gulp. Michael turned to the Librarian, shrugged and smiled weakly. Evie was not going to move and so, she was going to be part of this mission whether the men liked it or not.

Reluctantly, the other members of the mission team stepped onto the boats and sat down——Kerad, Essop and Lodie in one, Mikey and Evie in the other. Kerad and the boys looked at each other rather than catching the eye of Evie who was still seething.

The tension was broken with the sound of a child's voice. Tella was running towards the boats, calling out. Penny padded happily beside her chasing the strings of her smock.

"Wait, wait for me," she called. "I'm coming too." She ran and jumped from the quayside down into the boat landing safely in the arms of Mikey. Without hesitation, Penny followed her, leaping like a giddy gazelle. "Mikey, you love Lulu as much as I do so I thought we could share her." The child stared at him, wide-eyed. "Oops," she said," I mean Penny—— so we're coming along with you."

"No, no, my child," cried Malachi holding out his hand for Tella to take. "You can't possibly go."

"Yes she can and so can I." Marta, her mother sauntered to the edge of the quayside defiantly in full view of all the menfolk and began to climb down into the boat. "Evie is right. There's nothing to stop women being equal to men in the Coreland. Let's go and make a difference." Evie stood and embraced her. Several women shouted their approval in the crowd and so too did some of the men.

And so the mission team was complete: men, women, children and dog.

The boats pushed away from the marina to the sound of glorious cheering coming from the dwellers of Vilurbus. It was comforting, encouraging. As they put a distance between them and the city, it was clear the cheering had turned into chanting once again. Only the faint sounds of one single word echoed across the dark water. 'Heartblazer...Heartblazer...Heartblazer' resonated in Michael's ears for the second time that day.

Chapter 19

The Merevark

They had been travelling for a few hours. Evie and Mikey took turns with rowing and sleeping. Marta was only too eager to help out as well and insisted the children get some rest. Both Evie and Michael found they were pretty exhausted and feel asleep with ease. The canal they were travelling on held some of the dirtiest water they had seen since their underground adventure had begun. They had been equipped with long, slender oars that swept through the water easily for maximum speed. Every now and then, the oar dug up something foul and cruddy that stuck to its end and had to be forced off with vigorous shaking.

"How big is the Coreland?" Mikey asked Kerad. The man nodded slowly and pulling on his oar said, "Big enough." And that was the end of the conversation according to Kerad——he was strong and he most definitely was silent. The outspoken Essop didn't wait a heartbeat to give his opinion on the size of the Coreland.

"No one really knows how big it is or how far it stretches," he gabbled, "but there is one main canal that heads away from Vilurbus and we'll be turning onto that in a minute. We are pretty sure that if we follow the Great

Canal we'll eventually see signs that we're getting near The Mayoress." It seemed like he didn't stop to breathe. "The first signs would be an increase in the amount of pyrats about as Fester, the chief rat is always trying to please her and so he sends his subordirats to work for her. I don't know why he does it for I've heard that he gets nothing in return from her."

"How long before we get near to her do you think?" asked Evie as conscious as ever about getting home. *My parents will think I've vanished into thin air,* she thought, *or worse yet, be actually dead!*

"I reckon about a day's travel" said Lodie in his thin, squeaky voice.

"Could be longer though," offered Marta. Kerad coughed and stretched his neck either side to avoid it seizing up.

"We'll have to wait and see," he growled.

The boats glided down the waterway together and eventually veered left to enter the Great Canal. It was a vast stretch of water as wide as a football pitch was long. Their little boats seemed lost and quite insignificant in such an expanse. The ceiling of the tunnel was covered with luminobes all feasting on tangleroot and sticky boulic tubers. They marked out a pathway of neon-bright beads of light the length of the tunnel and as far as the eye could see. It was rather comforting to sail up the canal under their gentle glow.

They had been moving along for what seemed like hours under the steady navigation of Kerad rowing one boat and Evie rowing the other. The rest of the crew had fallen asleep one by one. Tella was the first to go. This had been quite a day for the little girl and she was exhausted. Mikey had tried to sleep but couldn't; instead he recalled how he had changed her life by returning her sight to her—both exciting and scary at the same time. Her mother, Marta was eternally grateful to him. *Maybe that's why she felt compelled to come and help out on the mission.* He wondered did she also come to make a stand for the women of the Coreland—all the women of the Coreland deserved only good things. All of them, except one—The Mayoress. *What kind of woman must she be to allow the dwellers to suffer? What gave her the right to be so mean, so selfish? What gave her the right to steal Dublin's water?* Truth be told—Mikey was scared. He needed to know that he could stand up to her…or at least try to. *How powerful was she, could she actually be stopped?* He was rather panicked about his core energy too. He still didn't know how it worked and all these people were relying on him. 'Mikey Heartblaze', they had started calling him. What if his heart didn't blaze?

What if he failed?

Thud! Michael was forced to stop his dreaming and fully focus on his surroundings. He couldn't row. His oar was stuck fast. The boat had collided with something under the water. He peered over the side. The water was moving a little faster now and was awfully cloudy——nothing visible at all.

"Hey," he cried to Kerad who was ahead of him by a couple of strokes. "I've hit something. The boat is stuck here. I can't move it."

"Have you tried using the oar to push off the bottom?"

"The oar's stuck in something."

"What about the second oar, try that." Kerad was drifting away faster now and he had to shout. Michael rooted out the second oar from the darkness of the boat and in doing so woke up Evie.

"What's going on?" she yawned.

"Here, take this and help me. The boat's stuck on something." The pair of them plunged the oar into the canal together. They pushed firmly, their faces going red, their knuckles turning white. With tremendous speed, the oar was whipped from their grasp and disappeared beneath the water's surface. They stared at each other, their mouths agape.

It started first as tiny, circular ripples that streaked and broke the surface of the water. Soon, the ripples turned to waves that chased each other, circling around the boat, steadily gaining speed. Evie and Mikey were knocked down and landed on their sleeping companions as the boat began to spin like a child's toy windmill. The surrounding flow of water was now a destructive vortex. Kerad and the others kept their distance and while they wished to help they dared not venture towards the danger. Tella screamed.

"Grab onto something that floats," yelled Michael to his shipmates, "in case we capsize." No sooner had he given the warning than the boat started to rock and shake until it finally flipped, tossing its occupants into the dangerous whirlpool.

The group were collected together in the spinning flow of water. Black bubbles rose and broke above the surface. They fought to keep their heads up; Penny doggy-paddled for all she was worth, Mikey held Tella up as best he could. *I can't hold on much longer*, he thought, *I'm slipping under.*

Some distance away, Kerad and the boys watched, completely helpless. Kerad knew of only one thing that could have caused this vortex—a merevark. He hoped he was wrong since merevarks were hideously sly and ruthless creatures. His suspicions were confirmed when he caught sight of the creature's gangly tail rising ominously out of the canal and then crashing back beneath the scummy surface. He wondered how he and the boys could help when suddenly that same tail swept past their boat just missing them by millimetres.

"Quickly boys, crouch down. It's too dangerous to stand up." The boys and Kerad knelt, tucking their heads down low. The merevark's tail was on the move again, sweeping cunningly, skimming the water, getting closer and closer to the boat. When is seemed like it was going to strike for a second time, it didn't; it pathetically wriggled to a stop and splashed into the watery darkness.

As quickly as it had begun, the vortex slowed its pace bit by bit and to everyone's relief, stopped. There was stillness all around. Evie managed to swim to the upturned boat which was a little bashed but still floating. Coughing up water as she went, she pulled herself up and held out a hand for the others. Tella was lifted up to safety. Mikey and Marta scrambled up after her. They searched the water for Penny; *where had she got to now?* The clever canine had managed to paddle to the water's edge and was shaking herself dry.

"Are you okay?" yelled Essop from the other boat. Mikey gave him a thumbs-up while he caught his breath. Kerad and the boys rowed towards them, their faces looking positive in the knowledge that nobody had drowned. Distracted and tired, they forgot the possibility that the creature could still be at large; they never saw the tail coming. The merevark, crafty and mean whipped its tail up and around the boat violently knocking its passengers into the canal.

"Oh no," screamed Evie in terror for she was yet to witness the creature, "there's something in the water!" Marta had her eyes fixed on the canal.

"Look!" she shrieked," the water is beginning to move again." The merevark was swimming, the water a minefield of roiling eddies. The whirling circle was wider this time; so wide that it sucked Kerad, Essop, Lodie and their boat into it as well. Now they were all flung together, whizzing around in a giant, frightening washing machine and it wasn't long before everyone slipped from their boats and into the water. The swirling got faster.

"I don't think I can hold on," screamed Marta. She was wildly spluttering water out through her nose. The party tried to grab onto to each other with Tella, Marta and Evie in the middle and create a kind of human raft but their concentration was all too soon shattered—a shadow darkened the tunnel. They looked up in horror at the figure of the merevark emerging from the canal. It looked like a cluster of bony tent poles, bending and folding with small, jagged spikes, shuddering as it rose to its full height. A noxious gas quite like rotting cabbages erupted from its ugly nostrils. It deftly enclosed the mission team in its serpentine tail. Wrapped up tightly, they were helpless, barely able to breath, let alone move. Penny barked at the beast; there was little else she could really do. Her noise echoed in her friends' ears, reminding them not to give up; there was always a way out, there was always hope.

"What on earth is this thing?" yelled Mikey trying his best to escape from the merevark's slimy grip.

"It's a merevark, a horrible creature. We have to try and escape as quickly as possible or we're done for," replied Kerad with real desperation in his voice. "If one of us can wiggle out of its tail grip and swim under it, it will loosen and give the rest of us enough room to slip through as well."

"I'll try, " cried Evie and she held onto Marta and Essop's shoulders and attempted to push down and away from them. Breathlessly, she struggled to slip free but it was no good—the grip was too tight. The mission team was truly stuck. They exchanged hopeless glances. What they needed was a miracle—and that miracle appeared just in the nick of time.

Speeding down the canal on a raft propelled by Dvarku stood a figure holding a large rock firmly at his chest. The direction and line of the raft's path was straight and determined and it moved like a torpedo, spraying up foam from its base. The glossum-powered vessel slammed straight into the groin of the merevark who was taken by surprise. The wretched creature faltered a little.

Turning swiftly, the raft spun around ready to attack again. Through the splashing water, Mikey and Evie could make out the grave face of Dmitri. In his arms he held a boulder and using a powerful chest pass, threw it at the merevark. It hit the monster right in the gut. Slam dunk! The creature groaned and with a quick turnabout, Dvarku drove the raft back around to face the merevark again. Dmitri was poised and ready to launch another thick rock. This time, he really made his mark and the merevark's tail started to sag. The prisoners didn't waste time; they swam out of its coils, making their way to the bank.

Kerad and Mikey were first to reach the water's edge and helped the others up. Evie was lucky enough to retrieve two catapults from one of the boats and it wasn't long before a shower of rocks was hurtling towards the merevark from the bank. Out in the middle of the canal Dmitri and Dvarku outwitted the creature's movements and struck it repeatedly with more rocks.

With accurate pounding from all sides, it wasn't long before the merevark had had enough of the onslaught and retreated noiselessly up the canal in the direction it had come. They group cheered then collapsed on the bank, happy to be alive. They were saved—saved by a glossum and a rather unexpected hero.

Chapter 20

Return of a Friend

Mikey and Evie were lost for words. Soaked through and bewildered, they just sat there shaking their heads. *How, when, why?*

"Here I am!" announced Dmitri, his arms open, his palms raised up in what you might call a ta-dah moment. On his face a big smile— so big in fact that it seemed like he had just swallowed a whole banana, skin and all. Evie spoke first, "How did you find us? How could you possibly know where we were?" Dmitri was about to answer but was interrupted by Michael.

"Why are you here?" He fixed his eyes on Dmitri's grim-looking face.

"I've just saved your life Michael, and that's the first thing you say? What is your problem with me?" Mikey said nothing. "Here's your camera. I found it washed up near a pool on my way here. Although, I don't know why I bothered." Dmitri shoved the camera at Michael.

"Thanks," he mumbled at the ground, turning his back to the group.

Evie gathered her wet hair up and tied a grubby bobbin around it, pushing the knot high on her head.

Dmitri stood before her with the glossum perched upon his shoulder.

"I see you two have met," she joked.

"He rescued me more than once from a slumber pool," said Dmitri, "and he's been at my side ever since." With admiration in her eyes, Evie patted the glossum's head and smiled.

"Well," she said warmly, "it's so good to see you. Tell us everything. How did you find us?" Mikey raised his head a little, listening carefully but still keeping his back to the others.

Dmitri introduced himself to everyone and told the group about how Dublin was badly in need of water as it was all being drained away and things were getting really bad. "People could die!" he reported, "the city is in a crisis." He told Evie how worried her parents were and how they should all return to Dublin as soon as they have fixed things in the Coreland. Evie's heart lurched at the thought of her parents. How she longed to be homeward bound soon however, right now she was enthralled by Dmitri's presence and hung on his every word.

"Tell us how you got here," she squealed, giddy to hear the tale. Dmitri took a belly breath.

"I have known about this place for a few years now. My granddad used to tell me stories about it but I was never really sure if he was telling the truth so I finally decided to do some research. I spent some time in the school library looking for clues; there are lots of books there all about local history." Mikey sat up suddenly. *That's why Dmitri was in the library.*

"One day I found a book that spoke of the opening in the Liffey wall and of culverts and tunnels beneath the city. I tried to take the book home to study properly but old Sykes wouldn't let me. He told me certain books needed to stay in the library. I tried to ask Meehan and the other teachers about it but they didn't take me seriously and just wouldn't listen."

"Why would Sykes care if you took a book out?" asked Evie, "he's a caretaker not a librarian."

"He's just a mean, old man, I guess," said Dmitri leaning against a rock. He paused for an instant, catching his breath. Evie watched his every move, her eyes fixed on his face.

"Go on, go on," she said, "don't stop."

"It wasn't until that day on the boat trip when we saw those crazy frogs, that I knew I was onto something," continued Dmitri quite enjoying his storytelling. "What my granddad had told me was really true. That this world really existed and the way in was through the grill in the Liffey."

"But, how did you know that we were here?" asked Mikey, a smidgen of interest in his voice. Dmitri swivelled around on the rock to face him.

"I was at your Mum's house. She was upset. Your parents were there too Evie, everyone is looking for you two. We were being questioned by the Gardaí. There is a search team looking for you now."

"Down here, underground?" said Evie.

"No, above ground in the city, they have no idea you're down here."

"But how did you know we were here?" repeated Mikey, his sullenness slowly vanishing.

"I remember your Mum mentioning that wherever you had gone you had taken your camera so I figured after you had seen those frogs, you wanted to go and get a better look at them through the hole in the river wall. Then when I heard Evie had gone missing too, I knew for sure. It took me a while to build up the courage to come down here but then I just went for it."

The audience listened intently to the story, questions building in their heads.

"Where did you meet the glossum?" Marta asked. Dvarku scampered up onto Dmitri's shoulders again and lounged there, curled up like a scarf.

"This little guy saved me from one of those dangerous slumber pools. I was drowning and sinking fast."

"He did the same for us," said Evie. "We both fell in and were nearly finished."

Michael walked towards Dmitri and Dvarku, his face more cheery, more positive. He reached out and stroked the glossum.

"Thank you," he said to the creature, "thank you for saving us all. Slumber pools are dangerous. If it wasn't for you, the three of us wouldn't be here." He gestured his hand to Evie and then back to Dmitri. Dvarku raised his sleepy head and gabbled in his usual manner.

"That's quite all right, you're all very welcome. I simply couldn't have you all drowning, apart from being a terrible thing to happen to anyone, if you had sunk to the bottom of that pool and were never seen again, who would we rely on to defeat the Mayoress and complete this quest. Really, it should be us that are thanking you." The rest of the group muttered their agreement. Even Kerad nodded with enthusiasm.

Mikey listened to the words with pride. He felt different. With his eyes shining and his head upright, a change had come over him and he showed his respect and friendship to Dmitri by offering him his hand. Without any reservations, Dmitri shook it solidly.

"I'm sorry for being an idiot," said Mikey, "I'm sorry for the way I've treated you— for how I've always treated you. Can we be friends?"

"Sure Michael, I'd like that." The two grinned at each other while Evie looked like she would burst with joy.

"Yes," she hollered, "hurrah for friendship!"

As before, it happened without warning; Mikey's heart lit up and glowed gently.

"Quick," shouted Marta, "the elixir! We need to activate it!" Mikey took the jar from his pocket and thrust it into her hands.

"Shine as hard as you can Mikey," Dvarku instructed. The boy tried his very best. His heart flickered and just like a lightbulb gaining a surge of energy, it became brighter. The mysterious rays pierced the gloomy cave spectacularly in a shower of gold. Marta placed her hands in the beams and the jar caught the light.

"You've got to really remember what you're feeling right now," whispered Essop with wonder in his voice. He pointed at Mikey's chest, "if you learn how to summon and control it, we can use it to defeat her."

"But do you really think I can?" said Mikey.

"You don't know the power of your good qualities Mikey," reminded Dvarku, "this light has the power to do wondrous things".

When the light dimmed Dmitri slapped Michael on the back playfully.

"Well done Mikey," he said grinning, not as amazed as he should be. "Dvarku has told me all about your incredible gift."

"Thanks a lot," said Mikey, feeling shy but ever so proud.

"Oh!" said Dmitri, "I almost forgot, I found this too. I think it belongs to you." He held out the dirty remains of Michael's cap. It was soaked through and looked nothing like a cap. Michael unfurled it and with hesitation, gripped it, deciding whether to wear it or not. He fondly remembered wearing the cap while attending a Gaelic football match with his dad. After a heartbeat, he stuffed it into his pocket.

"Thanks," he exclaimed, patting Dmitri on the shoulder.

When everyone had calmed down after Mikey's lightshow, Kerad suggested that they find a spot to camp in as they surely should eat and rest for a bit. They retrieved the one remaining boat and Dmitri's raft, tied them up and marched off to find somewhere safe and dry.

Chapter 21

Polander Flowers

Fortune was again smiling on the mission team for within minutes they had found a large clearing in a dry cave. It was decided that Kerad, Evie and Dmitri would go and forage for something to eat while Michael and Lodie would search for dry tangleroot with which to start a fire. Tella, Marta and Dvarku would remain to set up the camp and to gather as many luminobes and firemoths as they could. They all agreed not to stray too far from the camp spot and not to be too long gone; the last thing they wanted was for someone to get lost. Goodness knows what other dangers lay in these hidden passages and caves, another merevark perhaps. It was safe to say, nobody wanted to encounter a merevark ever again.

With a grubby, glass jar fluttering with firemoths to guide their way, Lodie and Mikey set off down one of the narrowest tunnels that led from the rocky clearing. Lodie was in the lead, his footsteps sure and steady. The boy seemed to know where he was going so Mikey just tagged along behind him certain that they would eventually come across some suitable kindling.

After some time of wandering through maze-like passages they came to a wide, damp cavern. On the left of them were slender, crystalline stalactites knifing through the ceiling against a low-sloping wall. They hung there catching the light of the insects in the jar. Musical dripping echoed in varying pitches from a row of tiny waterfalls that trickled away from the ceiling and down the walls—finally entering flat, brimming rock pools.

There was an overpowering sweet scent on the air; it was like nothing Mikey had ever experienced before. A portion of the wall was completely covered in a mass of tiny white flowers. When Mikey stepped close to them to get a better look, it was as if they were alive, scrutinising him.

"What is it?" asked Mikey as he picked off a section of the plant and inhaled on the delicate blossoms. "They're polander flowers. They have an intoxicating smell which is pleasant enough but they say too much sniffing isn't good for you."

"Why, what happens?"

"I'm not too sure exactly. They say it affects people in different ways." Mikey sniffed at the flower once more. He briefly bumbled about, his legs wobbling under him. His senses got lost in the strange flower's scent and he struggled to think clearly. His vision became blurred. He turned his head looking for Lodie. The other boy was on his knees, scrounging through the dirt.

"There's usually a better chance of finding dry tangleroot at the edge," he said, "where the floor meets the walls." The boys wandered around and found a wall each to examine.

While pulling away at dry roots Mikey fought to follow his thoughts. They all had become to merge. He knew he was lucky to be alive. That animal—that merevark was vicious and wasn't going to spare them. *Thank goodness Dmitri and Dvarku had appeared.* Dmitri had spoken about Michael's mother. *She was there too, escaping from the boat. Or was she? No, she was in Dublin with the Librarian, wasn't she?* He had forgotten how worried she'd be not knowing where he was. Mikey shook his head trying to make his eyes adjust but they remained cloudy. *Hello Mam*, he murmured, reaching out to take her hand. *I'm so looking forward to getting home to you. I miss you. Don't worry though, Dmitri is here now to help us get back safely.* Michael was pretty chuffed he had made it up with Dmitri; he hated fighting with people, really he did. He realised getting on with people was a much better life plan. He decided to make more of an effort with everyone he met. He glanced at Lodie, thinking, *I'm going to start with you.*

Mikey staggered toward him.

"How are you getting on?" Lodie hadn't found as much tangleroot as Mikey and was attempting to pull a thick piece that was wedged in a narrow crack.

"I've found a little bit here," he replied in his tiny voice. Mikey reached down to help him. His small hands had gone white from squeezing the root too much. The root was stuck tight but there was enough of it to wrap around your fist so both boys pulled as hard as they could, not to be beaten by the plant. With a snap, the root came free and the release sent Mikey and Lodie falling backwards. Lodie landed on top of Mikey, their noses almost touching. Lodie's hat had fallen off and Mikey spotted a decorative comb crafted from amber pinned in his hair of which there was an awful lot. Mikey reached up and took the curious object. Lodie's hair tumbled down, wisps of it landing on Mikey's face. He lightly brushed the hair aside and with hazy eyes stared at the face like he was gazing at a portrait in a gallery. *Lodie's sparkling, eyes, Lodie's rosy lips, Lodie's smooth, pearly cheeks, Lodie's long, silken hair—Lodie is a girl!*

His brain sparked into life. Mikey jumped up sending the pretty girl (who was no longer Lodie), rolling onto her back. He stood over her, equally dumbfounded and mesmerised.

"Who...who are you? You're a girl...I know that. I can see that but... who are you? You're not Lodie, who are you?"

"Take a breath," whispered the girl. "Calm yourself and I'll explain." She knelt at his feet and beckoned him to join her on the floor. "My name is Eodil, not Lodie and yes I'm a girl." Mikey sat down, all the while careful not to get too close.

"Why are you dressed as a boy?" he asked. The girl's big eyes danced in her head, her eyelashes beating open and closed.

"Didn't you hear what happened with your friend Evie and the dwellers?" Mikey nodded remembering Evie's standoff with the men of Vilurbus. "I wouldn't be allowed to go because I'm a girl and I really wanted to be here." Eodil smiled sweetly and took Mikey's hand in hers. "Don't tell the others, please. I want to stay and help. If they find out about me, they'll send me home." Mikey agreed with a curt nod of his head. He found he was a little lost for words when speaking to this girl; he was so taken with her beauty.

Eodil made her way over to the polander flowers and nestled down between the blooms. They made a soft cushion in a world that was mostly made up of rock. She gingerly patted a spot beside her.

"Come and sit down," she called. "Tell me all about *your* world." Reluctantly Mikey sat and shared and before long the two were chatting and exchanging stories about the Coreland and Dublin. Mikey found that he was enjoying talking to the girl and he forgot about why they were in the cave at all. He lay back in the flowers with his hands behind his head. Eodil began to tidy her hair using the amber comb. Fascinated by the movement of the lustrous strands of hair, Mikey watched in wonder, his pupils fixed steady, his breath suspended in his lungs. When Eodil was finished, she yanked up a clump of polander flowers and thrust them with little grace, into Mikey's face.

"Try them again, they're simply wonderful. They say every time you sniff them, you get something new and exciting— a scent more wonderful than the one before." Mikey inhaled two, three, four times. The flowers' strange perfume had captured his senses and his memory and it wasn't long before he was held in a trance.

When Eodil was satisfied that Michael had no real knowledge of what was happening, she reached into his tracksuit jacket and pulled out the small, glass jar of cleansing elixir the librarian had given him. She threw the jar onto the rock pools where upon it shattered. The precious liquid leaked out and was washed away. From under her belt, she produced a similar jar and placed it in

Mikey's pocket. The jars looked the same but the new jar held a completely different mixture.

Eodil hastily tied up her hair, replaced her large hat and finished completing her disguise as Lodie. She then shook Mikey awake.

"Come on," she said deepening her voice as best she could, "the others will be wondering where we are." A groggy Mikey came to immediately, an expression of confusion painted across his face.

"How long have I been asleep," he asked wearily. "Only minutes. When you had gathered all that tangleroot you said you were going to take a rest, next thing I knew, you were snoring so I left you and finished collecting on my own."

"Wow, feels like I've been asleep for ages. I'm sure I was even dreaming."

"What about," asked Lodie casually, "…..a girl?" Michael turned to look at the other boy, perplexed. "Yeah," he answered, "how did you know?"

"Lucky guess!" said Lodie smirking with mirth. "Let's get back to camp now. We should hurry, we've been gone for ages." He grabbed the jar of firemoths and headed for the exit of the cave. Mikey hurried after him, a stack of roots under his arm, the scent of polander flowers lingering in his nostrils.

Chapter 22

The Giant Pump

Like a troop of tireless ants Evie, Dmitri and the others busied themselves setting up camp. The first job was to light a fire. Kerad pulled a piece of flint from his coat and began to strike it against the blade of a knife in order to make sparks. After a few goes, the dry tangleroot took hold and with a little fanning, was set alight. The fire blazed brightly, a welcome sight for the weary travellers. Evie placed a scrawny clingfish on the end of a wooden spike and wedged it between two rocks. She positioned the fish over the flames so it would char evenly.

"I reckon we should eat and rest for a while and then set off again. The longer we spend here, the more precious water the Mayoress can ruin."

With their bellies full and their bones rested, the little group sat in a circle to discuss their next move.

"How far do we think we are from the Mayoress's hideaway?" asked Dmitri, "I am fired up and ready to take action."

"Given the amount of rat droppings in these caves, not too far I would say," answered Kerad, picking his front two teeth with the end of his nail.

"When should we use the cleansing elixir?" asked Mikey. The group remained quiet, contemplating this question for no one really knew the answer. Then Essop spoke, "I guess when we find the source of the dirty water—it must be coming from somewhere and it has to be clean to begin with." Everyone nodded. Kerad stood up and stretched his arms.

"Look, we'll know what to do when the time comes; we're armed with catapults and the elixir is now ready to use."

"We also have Mikey and his core energy," said Marta hopefully. Again all eyes were on the ordinary boy from Dublin.

"I'm still not sure how to...eh...use it," he replied with uncertainty in his voice.

"Well you had better learn quick," snapped Evie, "we may need your magic light—you just never know."

Now down to only one boat and a raft, they did their best to fit into the vessels comfortably and with vigorous strokes they were on the move again, sailing deeper into unchartered waterways.

After a while, the canal narrowed and abruptly came to a fork where it split into two smaller canals. The group were met with a decision—to take the right or the left canal.

"We should take the right one," shouted Lodie at Dmitri who was now rowing the raft.

"Why?" asked Dmitri suspiciously, "have you been here before?"

"Eh...no, eh...right just seems like a good choice," said Lodie smiling.

"Well what does everyone else think?" asked Dmitri looking around at the puzzled faces.

"Just go right, don't bother asking them," called Lodie a little aggressively. Not liking Lodie's confrontational manner and certainly not a boy who took kindly to being ordered about, Dmitri never waited for further discussion and pushed the raft forward taking the left hand canal just to spite Lodie. Marta, with oar in hand, copied Dmitri also taking the left canal. Lodie grumbled something under his breath.

Little by little, the atmosphere along the canal changed. There was a sense of trepidation in the air. The very odour of their surroundings was dank and faintly putrid.

"Rat droppings," whispered Essop, "we're getting close."

"Oh rats!" mumbled Dvarku nervously, "he's right, I can smell them, we're getting close."

Before long, the rowers had to stop as the canal just came to a sudden end. Straight in front was a rocky bank. They hopped off the boats to investigate. The bank was big enough to stand on—about four people deep. It was bare and uninviting, its back wall reaching up to meet a low, grey ceiling. A glut of luminobes glowed in the corners, clearly marking the presence of a dead end—there was nowhere else to go.

"There must be a pathway or a passage somewhere," said Marta examining the wall carefully. Lodie had other ideas; this was not the right place. He knew of another place he should bring them. *But not here.*

"Maybe we should turn back, this isn't going to lead anywhere," he called out. Kerad had just walked the full length of the bank several times and couldn't find anything.

"Perhaps we should," he replied.

"Why would the canal just stop?" asked Evie, "canals always lead somewhere that man has an interest in. They're man-made after all. This just leads to nothing. It doesn't make sense."

"Evie's right," said Dmitri, "this is too strange—we've missed something. There has to be more to here than what we can see."

With Penny chasing at his heels Mikey jogged up and down the rocky wall studying it carefully from all angles.

"What if it's something we can't see," he said, "but is here all the same...under our noses."

"What do you mean?" asked Marta.

"Well," began Mikey, "there may be something very obvious right here but it's just hidden or camouflaged."

"It can't be in the rock, we've tried for secret doors and there's nothing there," called Kerad from the other end of the bank, still checking the wall for hidden corridors.

"What about the canal?" asked Evie, "the water is so dirty here, it could be hiding something."

"This is ridiculous," said Lodie, "let's turn back and take the other canal!"

"No!" shouted Dmitri, instantly liking Evie's suggestion and splashing straight into the canal giving no consideration as to how filthy it was, "let's check out the bottom of this canal." He waded through the crud, his hands searching. "We've come this far, I'll dive under and have a look, if there's nothing, we'll hop back on the boats and head somewhere else." Without waiting for a response to his suggestion, Dmitri dipped under the water. It seemed a reasonable proposal and everyone was happy with the decision—all except Lodie. Lodie held his lips pursed together as if they were shut tight with glue.

Dmitri was gone for several minutes now and the others began to pace about with uneasiness. *Where could he be, maybe he's found something?* Evie had turned pale. "He's gone too long, we have to see if he's alright, he may have bumped his head or something like that and be lying at the bottom."

"Okay," replied Mikey removing his tracksuit top, getting ready to plunge in.

The tension was broken with the return of Dmitri who surfaced from the canal like some giant whale, splashing involuntarily and sending sheets of water everywhere.

"Oh wow," he shrieked, "you won't believe what I've just seen."

"What?" they shouted together.

"I've found the place where they are draining the clean water from the streets of Dublin above. It's no wonder that soon there'll be no water left; all the pyrats are working together to get the job done. You all need to see this and we need a plan to stop it now."

"But where did you see all this?" asked Essop.

"There is a wide opening right where the canal comes to an end but it's underwater. You can't see it

unless you dive under——Mikey was right, it's just hidden."
Dmitri was pointing vigorously at the spot somewhere in
the murky water right next to where the canal met the
rocky bank. "Who's coming?" he asked with great
enthusiasm.

With very little discussion, it was agreed that
everyone would dive beneath the canal and sneak into
the hidden chamber. Dmitri led the way, the girls and
Dvarku went next, followed by Mikey and Penny and lastly
Kerad, Essop and Lodie. They resurfaced in a shallow pool
tucked away in the corner of a large cavern about the size
of an airplane hangar. The place stunk really badly.

"Oo, pooh," said Tella, pinching the end of her
button nose. Luckily, the pool was completely concealed
from the main part of the cave and they made their way
around the rocky fence that surrounded them on their
bellies to ensure they wouldn't be seen.

The cavern was floor to ceiling filled with pyrats all
scurrying about and from this new position the horrible
stench was even stronger and more off-putting. *Pyrats
were just hideous creatures.*

Piled against the wall were all manner of
objects——things the pyrats had stolen no doubt. Mikey
could see clothing and books, jewellery, paintings, bits of

furniture, different-sized wheels, twisted bars from cages and large and small earthenware pots.

Stretching across the ceiling of the cavern was a twisted network of dull, copper pipes that fed into a long metal pump. The pump was violently sucking the fresh, clean water from above the earth and sending it to a reservoir below. This reservoir poured into the nearby canal. It was clear to see that the fresh water didn't stay pure for long as hundreds of rats spent time using the reservoir as a toilet, putrefying the clean water and quickly turning it into something sinister.

The cave was dominated by a huge mill wheel, spinning round and round, powering the pump. Inside the wheel ran thousands of pyrats, each one on the same pathway, concentrating on the same destination but never getting anywhere.

"That's how they're taking all our water," Dmitri whispered, his eyes dark and furious." The city is dying up there with the need for water and these rats are stealing it and making it undrinkable—unsuitable for any living thing… and for no good reason."

"They're following the Mayoress's instructions. Fester, the leader of the rats does as he is told," answered Kerad.

"Well, we've got to stop them now," said Evie. "What's the plan?"

It didn't take long for the group to decide on the best way to tackle this problem. The plan was straightforward; stop the pump and try to destroy it then purify the water with the elixir. Working as a team, they allotted each person a job. If they all worked together the plan would work. Mikey looked down at his fingers nervously and chipped away at a cracked nail. *Here goes nothing* he thought.

The plan was on. Tella wandered out into the centre of the cave wailing that she was lost. She wore her mother's silver chain around her neck to attract the pyrats (who couldn't resist the chance to steal something shiny). She was doing a terribly good job of distracting the rats as they almost stopped running in the wheel, their red eyes fiery as ever. The curious ones hurried over beside her waiting to pounce and take the chain but they weren't given the chance; Penny and Dvarku rushed out and rounded up those thieving rats into a corner along with help from Evie and Marta who had used Kerad's flint and had assembled two large torches that blazed fiercely. The rats didn't care much for dogs nor burning torches so they didn't dare try and jump on the girls. Tella joined her mother and Evie and helped keep the rats at bay.

Meanwhile, in the shadows beneath the mill wheel, right under the noses of the pyrats, Mikey and Essop jammed rocks of different shapes and sizes between the edge of the wheel and the frame that held it up. Mikey signalled to Kerad to go ahead with the next phase of the plan and he, Dmitri and Lodie got their catapults ready. Kerad looked around for Lodie. The boy had suddenly vanished. *Where was that boy? Was he alright? No time to find out now.*

Kerad and Dmitri leaped off the low, rocky wall that had kept them hidden and charged forward. With their catapults held aloft, they placed rocks the size of grapefruits neatly against the piece of animal fur and pulled back the rubbery band that attached it to the wooden handle. Back, back, further until the band would stretch no more, then they let go and watched the missiles fly, smacking and crashing into the curved outside of the spinning millwheel. Their aims were good and in minutes they had made great damage—but the wheel continued to spin.

On the ground, Mikey piled up rocks on the inside of the frame that supported the wheel hoping to slow the machine down. Some of the rats had broken free from the circle where the girls were keeping them and now threatened to jump and gnaw at Mikey and Essop. Essop pulled out a leather whip from under his coat and began cracking it in the pathway of the advancing rats.

"Take that, you filthy beasts," he roared.

Not ones to give up easily, Kerad and Dmitri kept loading their catapults with ammunition. Heavy rocks streaked across the cavern hitting the wheel again and again. Eventually the structure slowed and began to crack. There was nothing the rats could do. They quickly abandoned the wheel and retreated to the depths of the cave to take cover. The girls stared as the wheel fell asunder and crashed to the floor scattering splintered wood and frightened rats in every direction. The boys managed to avoid the falling wood, leaping to safety behind the rocky wall. The air was filled with dust making it difficult to see. Dvarku used his spindly tail to brush debris from his coat. Evie and Tella kept the torches out in front of them to ward off the cornered rats.

"I think we've done it," spluttered Evie, waving her hands and trying to see the spot where the millwheel was. Mikey called out from the other side of the cavern, "You girls okay?" Penny heard his voice and immediately followed it bounding through the rubble and dust. Evie, Dvarku, Marta and Tella followed. Marta walked backwards still waving her torch to ensure no more pyrats were coming from behind.

The group reunited, overjoyed in their victory.

"We rock!" screamed Evie. When the cheering had stopped it wasn't long before they noticed the absence of Lodie.

"We must start looking for him now," shouted Kerad, "if the pyrats have taken him, we have a better chance of finding him if we set off immediately."

"Who saw him last?" said Evie pulling a strand of hair out of her eyes and tucking it behind her ear.

"He told me he was going to get the boats ready out on the canal, so that we could all make a quick getaway," said Dmitri.

"When was that?" asked Evie.

"Just before we made a run for the wheel with our catapults. He was right beside me and then he was gone. At the time I remember thinking, why would he get the boats ready when we hadn't finished the job here but I was too focused on getting those stinking pyrats to give it any more thought."

"We should head towards the boats and see if he's there. It is probably wise to leave anyways in case there are more pyrats about," suggested Michael.

Just as before, they dived into the pool and swam under the opening in the rocky wall, re-emerging in the canal. Evie was the first one through. She scanned every inch of the canal and rocky bank. Nothing. The others eventually swam through and in no time the whole group were bobbing in the canal and wiping dirty water from their eyes.

"Where are the boats?" asked Dmitri turning his head in all directions. The canal was empty. No boats at all.

"They're not here," replied Kerad, "and neither is Lodie."

Chapter 23

The Mayoress

Michael was confused. *How could a boy and a couple of boats disappear so quickly? What could have happened to them all? How was everyone going to get back to Vilurbus?* He was looking forward to going home as soon as he could. Evie splashed water in his face and he jumped out of his daydream.

"You okay?" she asked.

"I'm fine," he replied splashing her back playfully. Then turning and addressing the whole group he said, "Okay, what should we do now? We're stranded here. And where's Lodie? Maybe we should go back and look for him."

"We are not going back in there with all those disgusting rats," said Dmitri turning his nose up.

"You won't need to," came a voice out of nowhere. The group searched the walls all around them. *Who had spoken?* It wasn't a voice anyone recognised...or was it?

Overhead a doorway had appeared in the side of the tunnel. Alongside it was a crumbling parapet concealed from view—especially for those on the canal bank. The parapet was dangerously high and snatches of dust fell from its weak spots. The group climbed out of the water to get a better look. A beautiful girl with lustrous hair looked down on them. In her hair was a single, amber comb. She smiled sweetly.

"Hey!" shouted Mikey, "I know you." The girl gave him a cheeky wave.

"How do you know her?" asked Evie sharply.

"She was in the cave with me, I remember now, there were lots of white flowers."

"What white flowers, we didn't see any white flowers?"

"Probably Polander flowers," said Kerad, "beautiful-smelling but if you inhale too much of their perfume they can give you temporary amnesia."

How did she come to be in the cave with Michael wondered Evie. *Something is very odd here.*

Dmitri was staring up at the girl in a daze.

"Who is she?" he asked dreamily.

"That's Eodil," answered Kerad, his face turning grim, "The Mayoress's niece."

The words had hardly left his lips when another figure came through the doorway. Her shadow preceded her, its threatening shape stretched across the ceiling. She appeared. A scatter of rodents scurried out from behind her and waited at the edge of the rock. Penny growled. She walked tall and straight, her body resembling the

174

reedy cane made from twisted amber that she carried by her side. Her bat skin boots whined with each movement. When she spoke, her sharp, military-style voice shot through the cave like firecrackers bursting on Hallowe'en night.

"So, here we are," she began, "the marvellous Mikey Heartblaze. At last we finally meet. Do you know who I am?"

"Yes," gulped Mikey. He was still reeling from learning the truth about Lodie. He could barely hear the sound of his own voice. His fear was creeping up inside him and scratching at his throat to get out. He was face to face with the notorious Mayoress and although frightened, he promised himself he would not let it show. *If only we had the boats, we could get out of here.* He swallowed the fear and answered her in a loud, clear voice, "What have you done with our boats?"

"They've been destroyed so you wouldn't be tempted to escape," she answered pointing to a pile of flotsam floating at the canal edge.

"Why are you doing this?" A gnarly smirk appeared on her thin lips as she looked first at Eodil, her niece, and then at Mikey.

"Water is power, power is everything. I wish to be the sole ruler of the lands above and below the ground and when I control the water, I control everything. It's quite simple really."

"You're making life miserable for the dwellers and every living thing," called Evie.

"And Dublin is suffering too because of your stealing" shouted Dmitri, "we're running out of fresh water there. You have to stop, now!" The Mayoress struck the parapet with her cane and chips of rock crumbled down into the canal, "I'm only getting started," she screamed, "and there's nothing you can do about it."

She glared at the group with dark green eyes. "We've ruined your pump," shouted Essop defiantly, "so you can't waste anymore clean water." With that, a light turned on in Marta's head. Something made her think of the cleansing elixir in the jar. She had kept it safe since the light shone on it, activating it. Now that the pump was destroyed, the water could be purified. With rebellion in her eyes, she bent down and cracked the jar against the bank, shattering glass and spilling its contents into the canal water. There was a thunderous noise and the cave shook a little. A white haze materialised over the water and then quickly turned violet. The canal started to move. The swirling water quivered and weaved in and out of short figures of eight. *This didn't look like pure, clean water? Why was it a strange colour?* Suddenly, the Mayoress shrieked with laughter.

"Has your elixir not worked properly?" she mocked.

In the nick of time, Kerad realised what had happened.

"The water—it's a slumber pool. Look away quickly, cover your eyes." With her palms over her face, Marta called out, "How did that happen?"

"I switched them," called the pretty girl from high on the parapet. *Lodie!* Now it was all making sense. Mikey knew he had been played for a fool, charmed by a girl who then gave him amnesia for her own gain. *How could he be so stupid?*

"I can have a new pump built in no time and begin taking fresh water again from wherever I like," said the Mayoress confidently. "In time, I will control all the water and you will all be at my mercy. I will create slumber pools to use as my weapons for they hold more power than you know." Mikey's frustration was mounting. He hated being tricked.

"You! Lodie…Eodil—whatever your name is, you tricked me," yelled Mikey, "you changed the elixir for something else." The girl remained silent. The Mayoress spoke again, "Eodil was good enough to blend the formula for me. It turns ordinary water into slumber water; all it needed was some core energy which you provided for me Mikey. Thank you." She sniggered viciously and pointed her cane in their direction. No one moved or tried to say a word.

"Look at you all— you pathetic creatures, is that all the fight you have in you? I would have expected a little more than that."

Peeking through her fingers and making sure to look up and not down into the dangerous slumber canal, Evie's mind raced as to how she could change the situation for the better. She dared not try and run for it for fear of the alluring power of the slumber water. She could feel the catapult that was tied on her belt swinging by her leg and the large rock in her pocket. *Could I try for a shot at this evil woman* she wondered? *Take her down?* The Mayoress went on, "Fester and the rest of the pyrats will be here any minute, perhaps I'll allow them to drag you all away to some deep, dark cave where you can stay locked up as their play things." She raised her head and smiled, "here they come now."

Gliding down the river on a wide barge filled with fiery eyes were the pyrats. They came out of the darkness of the tunnel, their teeth gnashing wildly. Fester was at the helm, his one single eye blinking like a beacon. Not long after their arrival, other rats started to appear from out of the canal. They quickly clawed their way up onto the bank and approached the dwellers. There were now hundreds of them. *We're done for,* thought Mikey, *if only I could do something, but what?* His brain was ticking rapidly, searching for a solution, something to save them, anything. *What about the light, would that make a difference?* He wished he knew how to control it. He stared at his feet, lost.

Trying not to look at the water, the group huddled into a corner to defend themselves from the pyrats. That was Evie's chance to strike. She moved like lightning, grabbing the stone from her pocket and swiftly placing it in the band of the catapult. *You've a great aim. 'Girl power!'* she mumbled to herself. Then, she went for it. The stone left the catapult and flew across the canal at top speed. It collided with the parapet somewhere just beneath the feet of the Mayoress sending dust and stone flying. The parapet gave way. Eodil and the Mayoress lost their footing. Eodil stumbled onto her side, her screams echoing in the cramped space. Her aunt helped her up, ensuring she was alright. With loathing in her eyes, The Mayoress motioned at Evie with her amber cane.

"Get her!" she screeched.

The pyrats immediately leaped forward, their furry legs moving as one. There were dozens of them. They zigzagged up Evie's legs and crawled across her back, shoulders and head, her body buckling from their weight. The girl stumbled backwards, fighting hard to maintain her balance. Kerad, Mikey and the others could only watch helplessly as they were surrounded by Fester and an army of more rodents.

Penny barked and tried to race to Evie's aid but Kerad held her tightly by the scruff, worried for her safety. Evie stepped too close to the swirling water and sensing the danger, the rats all leapt off her. Completely knocked off balance, the poor girl couldn't help herself and toppled in. Splash!

Mikey was in shock. He took no time to think, he just bounded to the water's edge and plunged in.

"What is he doing?" yelled Dmitri, "they'll both die."

"Dvarku, you can save them, the slumber water doesn't affect animals," shouted Essop, his whip threshing pyrats in all directions.

Marta and Tella had started to climb the sides of the tunnel hoping there was some opening through which to escape. Dvarku was with them and upon hearing Essop's suggestion, leaped down from his spot on the rocky wall and dived into the canal to help. Unluckily he chose the wrong spot and was speedily apprehended by Fester and a host of pyrats.

"You've already ruined my plans for those kids once before by helping them escape," hissed Fester to

Dvarku, "you're not going to do it again." With that, he shot out his tail and wrapped it tightly around the waist of the glossum. A dozen pyrats took hold of Dvarku and dragged him back to their waiting barge. Pulling away frantically, Kerad couldn't hold her any longer and had to let go of Penny who leaped into the canal too.

The Mayoress watched the spectacle like a child at its first circus.

"This is too much," she said to Eodil almost clapping her hands with glee. "What an elegant, entertaining way to die. I couldn't have planned it better myself."

Eodil didn't like this. She had trapped Mikey to carry out her aunt's wishes but she never thought it would come to this—death. Time was running out for Mikey and Evie but there was nothing she could do, any move she made to help them and she would be punished.

Darkness suddenly came upon the tunnel, the spiralling rainbow of colour and light from the slumber water faded—even the luminobes' little lights went out. Confused, the rats stopped gnashing their teeth and became motionless. There was an eerie silence in the cavern, not a whisper was heard, only the sound of the water lapping against the bank.

Shooting out of the canal and illuminating the tunnel in a shower of glowing droplets and piercing light flew Evie. She landed neatly on the bank scaring half the pyrats away. She looked dazed, her eyes drooping, her mouth hanging open in surprise. She was alive. The piercing light grew stronger in intensity and was followed by a sinister rumbling that seemed to come from deep, deep below. With a massive gush, the figure of Mikey burst out of the water too. He landed next to Evie, the golden rays of light spreading out from his chest, his heart a glowing ember of coal visible through his clothing and skin. His face was stern, determination, passion and heroism written all over it.

"Shut your eyes," he quietly instructed Evie, "and don't dare open them until I say." Mikey deftly observed that Marta and the others, fearful of the slumber water, still had their eyes shut. He pointed at the Mayoress, "You're finished! No longer will you control and ruin people's lives." Mikey Heartblaze stood proudly in front of the woman and shut his eyes. The light from his chest became brighter and brighter, his heart turning white with extreme heat. The spreading light made the cavern walls dazzle. The entire tunnel trembled and a clear, shrill note whistled down the tunnel. The pyrats screeched and scurried away from the sound. The Mayoress and Eodil were not prepared for the force they felt as their eyes were blinded by the penetrating rays. Sticking their fingers in their ears, they fought to stay standing. The heat, the light, and the noise rose to the highest intensity imaginable and then as quickly as they had grown, they faded and then were gone.

From the parapet above them, the mission team could make out the figures of Eodil and the Mayoress faltering and trying to find their feet. Just like Evie before them, they lost their balance. Luckily for Eodil, she fell, palms first against the rocky wall and slid down it unharmed. The Mayoress was not nearly so lucky, she tripped clumsily and plummeted head first into the canal and the nasty slumber waters, her body quickly sunk to the bottom, unseen and unheard. Eodil picked herself up and retreated through a crack in the wall. She didn't look back.

"Evie, you can open your eyes now, you're safe. Mikey's voice was soft and soothing. He grasped Evie's head in his hands and kissed her gently on the forehead. She looked to the floor, embarrassed at the gesture. Dmitri approached them.

"What about me?" he goofed, puckering his lips. "What about you?" Michael retorted smiling.

"No time for joking," shouted Kerad, "we should get out of here. The pyrats could return. They can't be gone too far away."

"He's right," said Dvarku who was now free of the pyrats' twisted tails.

"Wait!" shouted, Evie. "I have something to do." She rummaged in her back pocket and removed a small jar, identical to the ones that had held the cleansing elixir and the Mayoress's slumber pool potion. Looking at the baffled faces she answered curtly, "Malachi gave me a second one to mind... just in case. I remembered I had it and held it out in my hands just now, keeping my eyes shut. I'm pretty certain the light shone through it. Let's see." She lifted off the lid and masking her eyes, poured the elixir into the slumber canal. The swirling and colour immediately stopped. Nothing else happened. Dmitri looked glum.

"Ah well," he said, "we tried." The others nodded their heads mournfully.

"Oh now, wait a second everyone, don't give up too soon, let's try it," suggested Dvarku sidling to the edge of the bank and leaning down to the water. He took a sip, then another, then another. With expectant faces the dwellers, Mikey, Penny, Evie and Dmitri all waited for the verdict. "It's perfect," shouted the glossum.

"It's worked!" They all reached down to the water, cupping their hands and drinking the sweet liquid greedily.

"It tastes so good, the purest water ever," said Marta shoving her palms into the canal for more. She reached in and to her surprise felt something furry beneath her fingertips; Penny's matted head popped up and she barked.

"Hey pal," cried Evie, "glad you're back with us."

"Do you reckon it has worked for every drop of water in the whole of the Coreland since all the canals are connected?" asked Essop.

"I don't see why not," said Kerad. Satisfied with that, the group patted each other on their backs for a job well done.

Their celebrations were interrupted by a low rumbling noise erupting somewhere under their feet. Kerad's eyes darted from right to left uneasily. "Let's get out of here," he said, "that doesn't sound too friendly."

Chapter 24

Water, Water, Everywhere

Nobody, least of all, Mikey actually realised how mightily magical the core energy that shone from his heart was; it was a combination of heat and light energy fuelled and driven by the most virtuous qualities of the human spirit all spun together and presented through a young boy who was a worthy individual to carry such a gift.

When Mikey selflessly dived into the slumber canal to save his friend he again beckoned the core energy but this time managed to direct it as he needed. Having spent about three to four minutes in the canal while his light was shining, a huge amount of core energy was distributed through the water. Just like the spreading capabilities of the cleansing elixir, the core energy shot out in all directions and quickly travelled to the far reaches of every tunnel and cavern that held water in the whole of the Coreland. Most of the core energy remained in the spot where Mikey dived in and it surged ominously causing vibrations; growing stronger by the second. Mikey and the others wasted no time in getting out of there. "We should get onto the rats' barge and paddle like we've never paddled before," shouted Kerad who sensed that something dangerous was about to take place. Penny growled softly and Tella patted her head in comfort. The water in the canal began to bubble like a popped bottle of champagne, fizzy and foaming across the surface.

It was a little bit of a tight squeeze to get everyone on board the rats' barge. Dvarku held on the back and paddled, his wiry tail lashing from side to side. Kerad and Dimitri used the oars on the left side of the boat, Essop and Mikey on the right. They were sailing away quite swiftly when the first eruption came; a huge bolt of water blasted out of the canal and crashed into the ceiling. It had such force that it bit into the rock sending shards of limestone across the air. A second tower of water exploded from the canal and a third and a fourth. There was so much water hitting the ceiling now that large chunks of it were coming away and tumbling into the water causing waves that bounced towards the mission team.

"Row faster," called Evie. She paused to look for something else in the boat to use as a paddle and found an old net attached to a length of wood. She ripped the net off and used the stick to prod the bottom of the canal and thus push the barge in the opposite direction. Any extra speed would help, as it looked like they could very soon be surrounded by gigantic waves.

The water was now bubbling madly and had risen above the bank. The vibrations continued making the flimsy barge shudder. Suddenly, the whole of the canal leaped up as a powerful pop went off. The wall that had hidden the millwheel cracked, trickles of water appearing here and there.

"Quick, quick," shouted Marta looking back, "it's not going to hold." And it didn't—the wall fell apart, exposing a thunderous lake of water that was moving forward and gaining momentum at each second.

"Look out," screamed Marta again, "there's a tsunami coming." Panic crackled through the team.

"Stop," shouted Essop, "wait, we can ride it rather than allow it to take us down." The group stared at him in disbelief. "We don't have any other choice. If we do nothing we'll drown anyway. We've got to try!" The others began to nod in agreement—they'd try anything to stay alive.

"We can do it, we just have to get the timing right." The water was bustling towards them.

Kneeling in a row, they listened to Essop, "When I say go, I need you all to fall forwards onto your bellies. If we brace each other, arm over arm and no matter what happens, don't move or panic, we have a good chance of sailing on the top of the wave." They dropped to their knees and waited for the signal. They waited; time seemed to stand still.

"Now, quick move!" shouted Essop. They thrust their bodies forward and lying face down they grasped their friend and held tightly.

The barge did indeed stay on top of the wave but it shot ahead at a tremendous speed. No one dared move for fear of tipping it over and being lost to the tsunami forever. It was a wild ride that twisted and turned and dipped and dived, the surge of water not sure where it was going. The passengers felt almost in a trance; they had no clue of what was happening as fear had taken over their minds. Where were they? When would it stop? Were they going to see the end or were they going to hit a wall and be turned into mush?

Somewhere along its journey the strength of the tsunami discovered a particularly weak spot in the tunnel and instead of moving forward, it changed course, moving upwards. The train of water sped up and up, its passengers hanging on for dear life. It carved its way through caverns, tunnels and culverts, moving greedily, making a path for itself until it could go no further.

The city of Dublin has many fine squares; Georgian in their design, they're lined with stout houses, filled with walkways and ponds and bordered by iron railings. The square in Smithfield is different——it is more like the large squares you would see in French or German cities; a flat plaza stretching long and wide out towards its surrounding buildings. It was in Smithfield during the Sunday horse fair that the tsunami decided to break from its subterranean prison.

The people and the horses that wandered around the cobbled plaza of Smithfield got quite a surprise. They could hardly believe their eyes. Stones and cement were sent flying up over their heads while a glorious bounty of fresh water exploded out of nowhere, sending the animals scattering in fright. The fountain of water sent its offering of purity and salvation to the drought-ridden town in a shower of sweet droplets. The horse traders and sellers danced and shouted and cheered, letting the water soak them to the skin. The horses drank from the many puddles that spilled and lodged in the cobbles.

As if the horse traders hadn't seen enough of a spectacle, a rickety raft of all things leapt from the hole and eventually crashed down, skidding to a wet stop.

Some gathered and stared at the unlikely bunch of people that lay shivering in the summer sun on top of a broken barge—hardly moving, but still holding their friend in a reassuring clasp. They sat up and looked around, bewildered.

"We're home," announced Evie grabbing Dmitri and Mikey around the neck and resting her arms on their heads. "We've made it... and we're all safe."

It didn't take very long for the police and fire services to come and oversee the events that took place in Smithfield that day. The geyser continued to spit out clean, fresh water well into the next day. The area was fenced off as the force of the water was so dangerous, however, that didn't stop the people of Dublin—they came to gaze at the tower of water, came to hold their heads to the sky and catch the little droplets on their tongues and came to dance and sing letting the fresh water soak their clothes and hair.

Evie, Mikey and Dmitri were wise enough to sneak off to a side street and find an isolated water service chute and quickly send Essop, Kerad, Marta, Tella and Dvarku on their way back to where they belonged before the authorities started asking questions.

There wasn't time for long goodbyes for they could have been spotted at any time.

"Good bye Mikey Heartblaze," said Kerad grabbing the boy by the shoulders, real pride in his voice.

"We're so glad you came into our lives," added Marta. Tella left her mother's side and looked up at the beaming face of Mikey.

"I've been thinking," she said, "I think Penny should stay with you. You need her to look out for you." Mikey nodded, a tear in his eye.

"Bye Penny," whispered Tella as the dog nuzzled her one last time, "come and see me again... and thank you for looking after me."

"Take care, you fine young people. We won't forget you. Thank you for everything you have done for us. You've changed all our lives." Dvarku bowed, winked and disappeared beneath the street. And just like that—their friends were gone.

Epilogue

Within 24 hours of the defeat of the Mayoress and the return of the children to their hometown, fresh water flowed from the taps in Dublin. With the end of the drought, the crisis was finished and life could return to normal. It cannot be denied that the inhabitants of Dublin learned (although in the toughest way), the importance of water and how it should be cherished, conserved and never taken for granted. It was safe to say the landovers of Dublin used their water more wisely from that day on.

Dmitri, Evie and Mikey spent the rest of the summer in each other's company discussing their adventure, reliving it in detail and sometimes even wishing they were back in the Coreland. Often they had to pinch themselves that what they went through actually happened—it was amazing to think that below their city was a whole other, wonderful world.

Mikey's heart didn't blaze again that summer but his kindness never faded and his relationships with the people he loved never dulled or lost their sparkle; he was a changed boy. Mikey, his mother and Penny couldn't be happier. Mikey's dad did come to visit later that summer which was brilliant for Mikey but he only stayed for a little while. Mikey was okay with that now.

The children often wondered how Dvarku, Kerad, the Librarian and the rest of the dwellers were doing now that the Coreland had clean water once more. Their curiosity was quenched with regular visits from Parabisis who would croak outside Mikey's bedroom window eager to report news. As it happened, life below the earth was marvellous; a certain new joy flowed among the people, their lips still speaking of the children, their eyes still smiling from the cherished memories of Mikey Heartblaze and his friends and what those remarkable children had done.

On the day Mikey returned home his mother was preparing to wash his dirty clothes when she found his cap rolled up in his tracksuit pocket.

"Oh look, your cap," she said with surprise. "It looks pretty ruined. I think it will have to be thrown out." Mikey approached her and gently unfolded the cap. It's blue and navy colours had gone almost grey and it was fraying at the edges. The peak was bent now—gone was the attractive curve it once had, the Dublin crest faint, unrecognisable. Mikey Heartblaze held his cap tightly; it was a mature, well-travelled cap, a cap of adventure, a cap that had been through the mill. Mikey slowly lifted the lid of the bin and deposited the cap inside. His mother watched on silently, a little shocked.

"I'll have to get you another one," she said.

"No thanks," he replied, a crooked smile playing on his lips, "I think I can live without it. Besides, it only covered my face, covered my eyes——I prefer to be able to see all of the world round me because then you can be sure you never miss any of its wonderful possibilities."

The End

17857341R10121

Printed in Great Britain
by Amazon